"Don't you want to know why I'm here?"

"No, I don't," Mae retorted. "Anyway, you've obviously made a mistake and followed the wrong person. There's no way a newspaper would be interested in anything I do."

"You're right about that," agreed Lyndon Hyde. "But there is something about you that makes you interesting, Miss Stanfield."

Disturbed at hearing him say her name like that, she slowly swung back to face him.

"What else do you know about me?" she asked suspiciously. "Apart from my name."

"A good deal," he told her softly. "I can tell you the name of your father—if you want to know."

Mae briefly closed her eyes. If she wanted to know! It was the answer to the one question she had been asking all her life....

JOANNA MANSELL finds writing hard work but very addictive. When she's not bashing away at her typewriter, she's usually got her nose buried in a book. She also loves gardening and daydreaming, two pastimes that go together remarkably well. The ambition of this Essex-born author is to write books that people will enjoy reading.

Books by Joanna Mansell

Don't miss any of our special offers. Write to us at the following address for information on our newest releases.

Harlequin Reader Service
P.O. Box 1397, Buffalo, NY 14240
Canadian address: P.O. Box 603,
Fort Erie, Ont. L2A 5X3

JOANNA MANSELL

past secrets

Harlequin Books

TORONTO • NEW YORK • LONDON
AMSTERDAM • PARIS • SYDNEY • HAMBURG
STOCKHOLM • ATHENS • TOKYO • MILAN
MADRID • WARSAW • BUDAPEST • AUCKLAND

Harlequin Presents first edition August 1992
ISBN 0-373-11482-6

Original hardcover edition published in 1990
by Mills & Boon Limited

PAST SECRETS

CHAPTER ONE

MAE woke up just after dawn, opened her eyes, and wondered why she could feel a small shiver of apprehension running through her nervous system.

Then she remembered. It was because of the man who seemed to have been following her for the last couple of days.

She got out of bed, padded over to the window on bare feet and cautiously pulled back the corner of the curtain.

He was still there! Or, at least, his car was. A dark, shiny, very expensive piece of machinery—*not* the kind of car to drive if you didn't want to be noticed. He didn't seem to care if she saw him or not, though. He certainly wasn't making any attempt to be inconspicuous.

When she had first started to see that dark car wherever she went, she had thought it was just a coincidence. Or, perhaps it wasn't even the same car. Determined to be certain one way or the other, she had taken note of the distinctive number-plate—LAH 1. Next day, she had seen that number-plate again. It *was* the same man who was following her!

Her immediate impulse had been to go straight to the police. What would she tell them, though? That when she went to work, took her lunch break, or went shopping, an extremely expensive car always seemed to be parked nearby? It wasn't as if some seedy or obviously criminal character were following her. And he didn't try to accost her in any way, or even get out of the car to talk to her. He just sat and watched her.

Mae couldn't even give the police a physical description of this man who was showing such interest in her. The car had tinted windows, so she couldn't see the driver clearly. He was just a dark shadow sitting there, observing her movements.

Well, she was fed up with it! she decided with a sudden scowl. If this was the way he needed to get his kicks, by latching on to some girl and trying to scare her, then she *would* report him to the police. But first there were a few things she wanted to tell him face to face!

She hurried into the bathroom, took a very quick shower, and then pulled on jeans and a T-shirt. She didn't bother to comb her hair, but left it tumbling down her back in a cluster of wild dark red curls. A glance in the mirror showed her a face that looked a little pale, but very determined. And the odd yellowish hue of her eyes gleamed in the early morning light. Cat's eyes, she often thought to herself, wishing they were a more normal colour. Well, this morning she felt as if she had the claws to match!

Before she had time to lose her nerve, she left her flat, ran down the stairs and crossed over the road, to the black shiny car.

She still couldn't see the man inside clearly, but she was close enough now to notice one thing about him. He was asleep.

'But not for long,' Mae muttered under her breath.

She thumped very hard on the roof of the car several times, and had the satisfaction of seeing the man jerk violently awake.

When he saw her standing beside the car, he pushed a button inside the car and the window smoothly wound down.

'If you've damaged the paintwork, I'll sue you for the cost of the repairs,' he growled at her.

'And if you don't tell me why you've been following me for the last couple of days, I'll report you to the police,' Mae shot back at him. 'I don't like being tailed by a pervert!'

The only trouble was, now that she could see him clearly, she had to admit that he didn't look in the least like a pervert. He had dark, well-cut hair and, in contrast, very light blue eyes. Although a black stubble was beginning to show on his face, he was obviously usually very clean-shaven. More than that, though, this man was definitely sexy! Right now, Mae might be as mad as hell at him, but she could still recognise an outrageously unfair amount of sex appeal when she saw it. He wouldn't need to follow women. They would fall over themselves chasing after him!

Which made it all the more inexplicable why he should be so interested in *her*.

She began to glare at him again as she remembered how unnerved she had felt when she had realised she was being followed. 'You haven't answered my question,' she reminded him. 'I want some explanations—and fast—or you're going to be in serious trouble.'

The man began to lever himself out of the car, and Mae hurriedly took a couple of steps backwards.

'I've got a personal alarm in my pocket,' she warned him. 'Try anything, and I'll set it off. And believe me, it'll make enough noise to wake up the entire street!'

'I believe you,' said the man drily. 'I simply want to stretch my legs. I'm pretty stiff after sitting in that car all night.'

Mae didn't feel any sympathy for him. She did give a small gulp, though, as he straightened up. She hadn't realised how tall he was. He positively loomed over her, which made her feel intimidated, and she didn't like the sensation.

The man wasn't paying any attention to her at the moment, though. Instead, he was carefully examining the roof of his car, where she had thumped on it.

'Just a few dirty fingermarks,' he pronounced at last. 'You're lucky.'

'No, *you're* the lucky one,' Mae threw back at him. 'You're lucky I didn't kick a dent right in the door!'

The man shrugged, obviously unperturbed by her outburst. Perhaps he was used to threats. If he behaved like this very often, then he was almost certainly used to personal abuse.

Mae was feeling much more in charge of the situation now. For one thing, other people were beginning to appear on the street. She could see the milkman in the distance, a boy delivering papers, and a couple of people taking their dogs for an early walk. If this man tried anything, she could simply yell for help.

She took a couple of steps forward, planting herself right in front of him.

'I want to know who you are,' she told him in a fierce voice. 'Either you give me your name—and some proof of identification—or I'm going to send for the police.'

'You'll look fairly silly, if you do that,' he replied calmly.

'You think so? You've followed me around for a couple of days, and you've sat outside my flat all night. The police are usually pretty interested in men who behave like that.'

'Not if they're journalists.' He reached into his pocket, took out a wallet, and held it in front of her. 'This is my Press card.'

Mae stared at the card tucked into the front of the wallet. She had no idea what a Press card looked like, but she had the feeling that this was the genuine article.

'Lyndon Hyde,' she said, reading the name on it. Something clicked into place inside her head. 'And what does the ''A'' stand for?' she asked.

He looked at her blankly.

Mae pointed to his car. 'That is a personalised number-plate, isn't it? LAH 1?'

She put as much scorn into her voice as she could manage, but he seemed quite unabashed. In fact, he gave her a sudden smile, effortless charm oozing out of every pore.

'Yes, it is. I suppose that everyone's allowed one small piece of vanity. And the ''A'' stands for Alexander.'

'Well, Mr Lyndon Alexander Hyde, I've no idea why a journalist should be interested in me, but I do know that there's going to be a great deal of trouble if I see either you or this expensive but rather vulgar car of yours ever again.'

She turned her back on him and began to walk back towards her flat. Before she reached the front entrance, though, he called after her in a relaxed voice.

'Don't you want to know why I'm here?'

'No, I don't,' Mae retorted, without turning round. 'Anyway, you've obviously made a mistake and followed the wrong person. I'm a very ordinary person leading a very ordinary life. There's no way a newspaper would be interested in anything I do.'

'You're right about that,' agreed Lyndon Hyde. 'But there is something about you that makes you interesting, Mae Stanfield.'

It definitely disturbed her to hear him say her name like that. Slowly, she swung back to face him.

'What else do you know about me?' she asked suspiciously. 'Apart from my name?'

'A great deal,' he told her softly, his light blue eyes deepening in colour, as if he was pleased he had forced a response from her. 'I know where you were born and where you went to school. I know that you're twenty-four years old, and that you had a birthday three weeks ago. I can tell you how you got your first job, and where you now work. I know you've no brothers or sisters, there's just you and your mother. She lives in Kent, and you go down and see her at least once a month.' His eyes became more intense, and Mae shivered, although she didn't know why. 'I know the name of every boyfriend you've ever had, although there have been surprisingly few, considering your age. You don't seem very good at personal relationships, Mae Stanfield. Or perhaps you just like to keep your life uncomplicated.'

Mae was breathing hard by this time, and she knew her cheeks were glowing with bright colour.

'You've no right to know all those things about me!' she threw at him furiously.

Lyndon Hyde seemed unmoved by her reaction. 'There's nothing illegal about doing some detailed research into someone's life.'

'It might not be illegal, but it's certainly immoral,' Mae yelled. 'Although I suppose it's all you can expect from the gutter Press!'

'I don't work for the gutter Press,' he retorted sharply.

Mae realised it was the first time she had got through to him, and she felt a small surge of satisfaction. 'You certainly use gutter tactics,' she accused.

His eyes became a little harder, and it occured to her that it might not be wise to cross this man.

So, what was she supposed to do? she asked herself angrily. Just walk away without finding out why Lyndon Hyde had bothered to dig out all those highly personal details about her? Why he had probed so deeply into her life, when it was so ordinary that there were times when it was positively dull?

Yet, only moments ago, she had been going to do just that. What was now stopping her?

Something in that light blue gaze of his, she admitted to herself uneasily, at last. He had the look of a man who knew even more than he had so far admitted.

Mae suddenly had the feeling that she had reached some sort of crossroads. She could ignore Lyndon Alexander Hyde, walk on into her flat and pretend that none of this had ever happened. If she did that, her life would carry on as normal and nothing would ever change. On the other hand, she could begin asking more questions. Find out *why* this man had suddenly become so interested in her.

Yet, she was quite certain that was a very dangerous path to take. She couldn't have explained how she knew that. She was just very sure that this man had it in his power to change her entire life, turn her future—everything!—upside-down.

A sudden wave of cowardice swept over her. She didn't want her life to change! She was quite happy as she was, she told herself with some determination. OK, so nothing very exciting ever seemed to happen to her, but she could live without excitement. She had managed it for twenty-four years, hadn't she? She liked peace and quiet, she assured herself. Perhaps Lyndon Hyde was right, and that was why she hadn't complicated her life with any relationships that threatened to turn into something too serious. Maybe it was why she worked as a legal secretary, in a well-run and orderly office.

No, she decided firmly, she didn't want to know why this man had suddenly appeared in her life and made it his business to know so much about her. This was one instance when ignorance would definitely be bliss!

She began moving away again, resisting the unexpectedly strong temptation to glance back into those light blue eyes one last time.

'Walking out on me, Mae Stanfield?' Lyndon Hyde called after her softly. 'But I know things about you that you don't even know yourself. Aren't you interested in finding out what they are?'

Mae took a very deep breath. 'No,' she said, making her voice as decisive as she possibly could.

There was a brief silence, and for a few moments she thought he was actually going to let her go without saying anything more.

She was wrong, though.

'Wouldn't you like to learn the name of your father?' he said in a voice that was low and level, and yet carried perfectly clearly.

Mae felt herself go completely cold. She stood very still, and yet the pavement seemed to rock gently beneath her feet.

Very, very carefully, because the whole world suddenly seemed to be built on very shaky foundations, she turned round.

'*What* did you say?' It took an enormous effort to get every one of those words out, and an even bigger effort to control her suddenly trembling body as she waited for his reply.

Lyndon Hyde's blue gaze rested on her white face. 'I asked you if you'd like to know the name of your father.'

She began to recover just a little. 'Is this some sick joke?' she demanded tautly.

He shook his head. 'No joke. I can tell you—if you want to know.'

Mae briefly closed her eyes. If she wanted to know! It was the one question she seemed to have been asking all her life. The one question her mother had always flatly refused to answer—Mae didn't even ask her any more, hadn't asked her for years. And now this man calmly announced that he could tell her...

She shivered abruptly. Lyndon Hyde noticed. 'Shall we go into your flat?' he suggested.

'I suppose so,' she muttered shakily. And with those few words, she knew she had gone past the crossroads. Everything was starting to change, and she couldn't stop it. She couldn't even go back to the place she had been just a few minutes ago.

Lyndon followed her up the stairs and into the tiny top-floor flat, with its one main room that was both living-room and bedroom. He sat himself on one of her secondhand chairs, and somehow didn't look out of place despite his expensive clothes, gold watch and general air of affluence.

'Do you want me to tell you straight away?' he asked her. 'The name of your father?'

Mae wouldn't meet his gaze. 'No,' she said in a flat tone. 'I want some more information first. To start with, you can tell me why you were even interested in tracing him. I'm sure you don't make a hobby of finding the lost relatives of people you don't even know!'

His light blue gaze rested on her thoughtfully. 'I'm beginning to think that there are quite a few things I'd like to make a hobby of, where you're concerned,' he said. There was a rather different note in his voice now, and Mae had the impression that he was looking at her properly for the first time.

She had absolutely no interest in him, though, except for the information that he could give her.

'Just start talking,' she snapped, edginess giving her voice an uncharacteristic sharpness.

'All right,' he agreed, settling back into his chair and looking totally relaxed. 'To begin with, I didn't set out to find any connection between you and the man I believe to be your father. I didn't even know you existed, at that stage. This whole thing started when my paper asked me to do a detailed feature on your father——'

'Why did they do that?' Mae interrupted him.

'Because he's rather well known—some might even say notorious—in certain circles.'

'What kind of circles?'

'Financial circles,' Lyndon told her. 'When I tell you his name, you'll almost certainly recognise it.'

Mae swallowed hard. Part of her wanted to hear that name straight away, but another part, a cowardly part, wanted to put it off for a little while longer. She seemed to have spent most of her life waiting for this moment. Now that it was finally here, it was a lot harder to face than she had expected.

'What kind of feature were you going to write on him?' she asked in a low voice.

'A general coverage of his life, from his birth right up until the present. He came from a fairly poor background, and today he's worth—well, no one knows quite *how* much he's worth. A million pounds is probably small change to him, though.'

Mae blinked rather dazedly. This was getting harder and harder to believe. How could a man like that be her father? Lyndon Hyde had to have made some kind of mistake!

'Tell me more about this feature you're doing on him,' she said, trying to get him to talk some more so that she would have time to think. 'It sounds like a rags-to-riches story. That kind of thing's been done a hundred times before, though, hasn't it?'

'People are still fascinated in knowing how someone can start out with virtually nothing and end up with a vast fortune,' Lyndon replied. 'And yes, it's been done a hundred times before, but you can make it fresh and interesting if you use the right approach. And in the case of your father, his personal life is just as colourful as his financial dealings.'

Mae's yellow eyes abruptly began to grow cold. This was suddenly beginning to make a great deal of sense.

The man was a journalist, wasn't he? And, now-adays, a lot of journalists didn't seem to think it was necessary to stick to the facts. If a story looked as if it was going to turn out to be rather dull, then why not invent a few things to spice it up?

She looked at him accusingly. 'And is that what your article is going to concentrate on? His personal life?'

'The man behind the money?' He gave a small shrug. 'Why not?'

'No reason at all,' Mae retorted. 'Just as there's no reason why you shouldn't invent a few "facts" to make the story even more interesting. Digging up a long-lost daughter would give your story a *very* juicy slant, wouldn't it? What's the matter?' she taunted. 'Wasn't the feature turning out to be quite interesting enough? Did you need a nice piece of scandal to make it sell? Well, I don't know why you chose *me* to play the part of this man's abandoned daughter, but it isn't going to work, Mr Hyde! I don't believe a single word you've told me. I want you to get out of here right now, and if I ever see you again I'm going to tell the police that you're harassing me and have you slung in gaol. And if you print one single word of these nasty little lies you've invented, I'll sue you and your paper for so much money that you'll both be left without a penny!'

Her face and skin was burning hot now with the great wave of anger that had surged over her. She stood there, her eyes blazing at him and her whole body tensed into a totally belligerent stance.

Lyndon Hyde got to his feet, and walked over to the door.

'All right, I'll leave,' he said in a level voice. 'Perhaps I should have approached this in a different way. I should have realised this would come as quite a shock to you. But I want you to think over what I've said. And when you want to talk to me again, you can reach me at this number.'

He took a small white card from his wallet and placed it on the table.

Mae immediately picked it up, ripped it into pieces, and then threw it into the nearby waste-paper bin.

'I shan't want to get in touch with you,' she told him fiercely. 'And if I find you've repeated these sordid lies to anyone else or put one word of them into print, I'll cause you a great deal of trouble, Mr Lyndon Alexander Hyde.'

He had reached the door by now, but he stopped there for a few moments.

'Just remember,' he said in a slightly grim tone, 'you can only sue someone if you can prove that they've lied. And I don't think you'll be able to do that, Miss Stanfield. On the other hand, I'll be able to offer fairly substantial evidence that I'm telling the truth.'

And with that distinctly disturbing declaration, he closed the door behind him and left.

Mae sank down into the nearest chair. Quite suddenly, this all seemed to be too much to cope with. The man was lying, of course. He had to be lying, she told herself on a rising tide of panic. Because if he wasn't . . .

She quickly closed her mind to that particular train of thought. He was a journalist after a sensational story, that was all.

So, why pick on *her*? asked a small voice inside her head. Why sit outside *her* flat all night? Tell her that she was the daughter of this rich, powerful businessman who was going to be the subject of a lengthy and in-depth newspaper article? There must be thousands and thousands of other girls in London he could have chosen.

Mae grimly forced all the disquieting questions out of her mind and told herself she wasn't even going to think about it any more. She was going to get ready for work, and pretend that this was just a normal day.

She got up with fresh determination, stripped off her jeans and T-shirt, and instead put on a crisp white blouse and a neat dark suit. There wasn't enough time to do much with her hair. A few dabs of gel smoothed down some of its wildness, and she secured the dark red curls behind her ears with a couple of wide combs. Normally, she didn't wear it loose for work. The firm of solicitors where she worked as a legal secretary was very conservative. A tangle of curls hanging down her back would definitely be disapproved of.

'Well, they'll just have to put up with it for once,' she muttered under her breath.

A glance at her watch warned her that she was going to be late. She grabbed her bag, wriggled her feet into a pair of black, shiny shoes, and headed for the door.

She had actually got halfway through it when she suddenly came to an abrupt halt.

Who was she kidding? she asked herself with a resigned shake of her head. She wasn't going to make it into work today. Right now, her head felt too confused even to cope with the simple action of catching the right bus to take her there. She certainly wasn't capable of dealing with complicated legal documents, taking dictation, or even answering the phone coherently.

She kicked off her shoes again and sank back on to the chair. She would ring them a little later and tell them she wasn't feeling too well—which wasn't exactly a lie!

There was a small piece of white card on the floor and, after a few seconds, she picked it up.

It was a torn corner of the card Lyndon Hyde had given her. When she had chucked the pieces into the waste-paper basket, this bit had missed it and fallen on to the floor.

Mae stared at it for a very long time. Then, slowly, she retrieved the other pieces from the waste-paper basket and fitted them together.

There were two phone numbers on it: his home number, and the number of his newspaper. She saw that she had been quite wrong when she had accused him of writing for the gutter Press. This was a very up-market paper. It was also one that definitely frowned on sensationalism. Lyndon Hyde's article would need to be well-written, accurate and informative if it was to be printed by this particular paper.

Mae found that more than a little disturbing. It meant that Lyndon Hyde would have checked and re-checked his facts. And if he was quite certain that everything he had told her this morning was accurate, where did that leave her?

She sat there for another half an hour, just staring blankly ahead of her. She supposed she ought to be going over and over everything that had happened today, to try and sort it out satisfactorily in her own mind. Instead, the inside of her head seemed completely blank. She was incapable of any kind of logical thought or reasoning.

At the end of the half-hour, she saw her hand reaching out for the phone. It picked up the receiver; then it dialled one of the numbers on the card Lyndon Hyde had given her.

It was his home number. He won't be there, Mae reasoned with herself. He'll be at the paper, or out on another assignment. I'll let the phone ring a few times, then I'll put it down and forget about all this.

The phone was answered on the second ring, though.

'Hello?'

She recognised Lyndon Hyde's voice immediately. It had a very distinctive edge to it. No one else's voice would sound quite the same.

'Hello?' he said again, a little more impatiently. Then, in a rather different tone, he added, 'Is that Mae Stanfield? I've been waiting for your call.'

'How did you know I'd ring you?' she said after a long pause.

'This isn't the kind of thing you can just walk away from, is it? If I were you, I'd want to know more. *Need* to know more.' When she didn't say anything, he added, 'Do you want to come round?'

'I suppose so,' she muttered, with deep reluctance.

'Do you have a piece of paper handy? I'll give you my address.'

Mae scribbled it down. 'Will you be in all morning?' she asked.

'I'll wait all day for you, if that's how long it takes,' he answered in an unexpectedly velvet voice. 'Take a taxi. I'll pay for it, if you're short of cash.'

'I'll pay my own way,' Mae said stiffly. 'That's if I even come. I might change my mind.'

'I don't think so,' he said softly. And before she could say anything else, he put down the receiver.

Mae glared at the phone. 'I hate people who are always sure of themselves!' she told herself with a dark scowl. Then she twisted her fingers together indecisively. Was she going to go, or not?

A deep sigh finally escaped her. What a stupid question. Of course she was going to go. She couldn't spend the rest of her life wondering if Lyndon Hyde had told her the truth.

She rang for a taxi and, when it arrived, hurriedly scrambled into it before she could change her mind yet again.

It took her halfway across London, finally drawing to a halt in a small, quiet square. Mae had just enough money to pay the fare, but wasn't worried about how she would get home again. There were too many other things on her mind right now.

The square was ringed by large, elegant houses, and Mae's eyebrows gently rose. This was a pretty exclusive address. How much did journalists earn nowadays? Surely not enough to pay for this sort of lifestyle?

She soon found the number of the house written on the scrap of paper in her hand. According to the gleaming brass plate outside, Lyndon Hyde occupied the ground-floor flat. Mae pressed the bell, and his voice immediately sounded through the security phone.

'Come straight in.'

She felt like a very small fly being invited in by a smooth-talking spider. Nervously, she opened the door and found herself in a large, airy lobby.

The door to Lyndon's flat was opposite, and it stood ajar. You don't have to go in, she told herself. You can just turn round and go back home, if you want to.

Except that she couldn't. She knew that, and Lyndon Hyde knew it just as well. That was what gave him the advantage in this situation.

Mae swallowed hard, and walked through the door that led into his flat.

He was waiting for her, still impeccably dressed and looking even better groomed than before since he had shaved since she had last seen him. The flat had been decorated and furnished with perfect taste, and Mae couldn't help thinking that he blended in with his surroundings like a chameleon.

'Do you want something to drink?' he asked courteously.

'No, thank you,' she muttered. She walked restlessly to the far side of the room, shooting a quick glance at him as she did so.

Until now, she hadn't quite been able to remember what he looked like. She could only seem to recall small details. The light, clear blue of his eyes; the darkness of his hair; the texture of his skin; a faint male scent, musky and curiously pleasant, almost stimulating.

And when all those details were put together, the overall effect could easily have been quite staggering, in any other circumstances. Mae realised that this man was what her mother would call quite a catch! Except that he had almost certainly been caught by someone else by now. Men like that didn't roam around on their own for long. Females would be attracted in their droves, and they would simply pick out the one they wanted——

She realised that Lyndon was watching her rather speculatively now, and she flushed brightly, afraid he could tell what she was thinking. Worse than that, he might think that she was interested in him—and she most certainly wasn't! She had just been trying to distract herself from the real reason why she was here.

'Why don't you sit down?' Lyndon invited.

Mae was glad to take up his invitation, because her legs felt as if they might not support her much longer. She collapsed on to a sofa covered in soft cream leather, took a deep breath and then stared rather defiantly at him.

'I want more information,' she said bluntly. 'I'm not saying that I believe a single word you've told me so far, but I want to know why you think I'm this man's daughter.'

His blue eyes took on a brighter sheen. 'You still don't want to know his name?'

'No,' she said, swallowing hard. 'Only why you think there's some connection between this man and me.'

'All right, I'll tell you,' he said, sitting down in the armchair opposite her. Mae found her muscles were becoming locked rigid with tension, and she forced them to relax as he continued speaking. 'Before I begin work on a feature article of this kind, I always do a great deal of research. I don't always have time to do all of it myself, though, so I employ someone I know who's a specialist in this kind of thing. He digs out any facts that he thinks might be relevant.'

'Who is this person?' Mae asked suspiciously.

'He's a private detective,' Lyndon answered calmly.

She looked at him with some disgust. 'And that's how you get your background information on the people you write about? You employ a private detective to dig out all the dirt on them?'

'I use him only occasionally,' Lyndon corrected her, a slight edge to his own voice now. 'He has contacts that I don't have access to, he can get his hands on information that's beyond my reach.'

'And does he do this legally, or illegally?' Mae challenged him.

Lyndon smiled charmingly, but there was also a warning light in his eyes. 'I don't ask.'

'No, I bet you don't,' she muttered fiercely. She longed to tell him that she didn't want to hear any more of this, that the methods he used disgusted her, but this had all gone too far now. She knew that she was going to have to listen to everything that he had to tell her, no matter how much she hated it.

'All right, what information did this private detective dig up for you?' she asked, her brows furrowed together darkly.

'He managed to get copies of some very personal accounts, stretching back over quite a few years.'

'And you're not telling me *that* was legal!'

'Possibly not,' Lyndon conceded. 'But they were certainly very interesting. For a start, they told me that this man had been paying the school fees for a child who didn't seem connected to him in any way. I began to wonder why he would do that. And on top of that, he paid the medical fees for a minor operation for this same child. Did you have your tonsils out when you were nine?' he asked.

Mae found her throat was growing uncomfortably dry. 'Yes, I did. But that doesn't mean I was that child,' she added defensively.

'And did you go to a private school? Cranborough School?'

'Yes. But the fees were paid for out of a special fund,' she said quickly. 'It was some kind of scholarship scheme.'

Lyndon shook his head. 'There wasn't any scholarship scheme. Your education was paid for by your father.'

'Why would he do that, and yet never try to see me?' Mae muttered, still not wanting to believe any of this, but finding it harder and harder to do that.

'I don't know,' Lyndon replied frankly. 'That's something that we still have to find out.'

She didn't like the way he had said 'we'. It implied some sort of contact between them in the future, and she felt as if she had already seen more than enough of Lyndon Hyde.

'Do you want to know his name now?' he went on softly.

Mae licked her lips. 'I suppose so,' she managed to get out in a croaky voice.

'It's Malcolm Morgan.'

He was right, she *had* heard of him. Probably most people had. He had been behind a lot of very lucrative deals recently, attracting even further publicity because some of his business methods were thought to be highly unorthodox.

'I don't see how he could possibly be my father,' Mae said in a slightly strangled tone, after a very long silence. 'You've got to be wrong about this.'

'Do you know what he looks like?'

'I suppose I must have seen his picture in the papers. I can't remember any details, though.'

'A newspaper picture is nearly always in black and white,' Lyndon observed. 'Try looking at a colour photo of him.' He picked up a folder on the table and took out a large, glossy photo. 'This is Malcolm Morgan,' he said evenly, handing it to Mae.

She took it from him with unsteady fingers, and then just stared at it.

No wonder a black and white photo would have made no impression on her. You needed to see Malcolm Morgan in colour to realise that his thick hair was dark red, and that his eyes were a strange shade of yellow.

Mae had always known that she must have taken her colourings from her father. Her mother had light hair, and her eyes were an ordinary shade of brown.

'It's like looking into a mirror, isn't it?' said Lyndon in a quiet voice. 'As soon as I saw you, I knew that I'd put all the information together correctly, and that this man was your father.' Then his tone took on a rather harsher note as he continued. 'Malcolm Morgan is a powerful man, an influential man, a very wealthy man. He's paid for your schooling and your medical bills, and he seems to think that fulfils his obligations towards you. I happen to disagree about that, though. I think that it's time he was forced to acknowledge openly that you exist!'

CHAPTER TWO

MAE felt as if the inside of her head were spinning wildly. When she had first woken up this morning, her life had been the same as it had always been. Now, she knew the name of her father. She even knew what he looked like.

She no longer questioned the validity of Lyndon Hyde's research. The facts that he had dug up were true—she instinctively knew it.

The question remained now, what was she going to do about it?

Phone her mother? Confront her with the truth, and demand to know more about the circumstances of her birth?

But Mae didn't want to do that. Where the subject of her father was concerned, a great wall seemed to exist between herself and her mother. When she was younger, she had asked endless questions, and not one of them had ever been answered. She had tried tears, tantrums and pleading to try and squeeze some information out of her mother, but nothing had ever worked. Finally, she had stopped trying to find out anything about her father. She had known that she would never get anything out of her mother except for a chilled silence.

Now, though, she had been given a chance that she had never expected. She could find out for herself some of the answers to all the questions that had piled up inside her over the years.

She had the name of her father. And she had a picture of the face that went with that name. A face which uncannily resembled her own—something she hadn't expected, and found more than a little disturbing.

Lyndon had been watching her all through the long silence that had followed his last statement. He seemed to be waiting for her to digest everything he had told her.

'I can take you to him,' he said at last. 'That's if you decide that you want to see him.'

'If I want to see him, I can go by myself,' Mae said sharply.

'No, you can't,' he answered easily. 'For a start, you don't know how to find him.'

'That shouldn't be too difficult,' she retorted. 'He's a well-known man. It should be easy to discover his movements.'

'Not as easy as you seem to think. Well-known men are often harder to find than ordinary people. For a start, I can tell you that he's out of the country at the moment. He probably won't be back in England for two or three months.'

'I'll find some way of getting in touch and letting him know who I am,' she said hotly. 'He'll *have* to make arrangements to see me then.'

'Why?' asked Lyndon in a calm tone. 'For the last twenty-four years, he's virtually ignored your existence. What makes you think he's going to want to see you now? Once he finds out that you've discovered his identity, there's every chance he'll go to some lengths to make sure you never get near him. And he can do that,' he warned. 'He surrounds himself with a formidable barrier of secretaries, personal assistants and security men.'

'But you can get through them?' she said with some scepticism. 'You're saying that you're the one person who can get me close to him?'

'Yes,' he said in an unruffled voice.

'And what do *you* get out of it?' Mae challenged him. 'And don't try and tell me that you're offering to do this because you're feeling charitable!'

'Of course not. I'm doing it because I've put a lot of work into this project, and I want to see a satisfactory end to it.'

Mae's eyes took on an angry sheen. 'In other words, it would make a great angle for your article! You want to report the whole thing from beginning to end. How you found me, how you took me to my father, and what we said to each other at that first meeting!'

Lyndon shrugged. 'I'm a journalist. It's what I do— and I do it well.'

'Oh, you're very thorough!' Mae agreed bitterly. 'You do your research—with the help of some sleazy private detective—and you get results. But it's still a pretty dirty way of earning a living!'

He seemed unmoved by her attack. 'Do you want me to take you to Malcolm Morgan, or not?'

Mae wished dearly that she could tell him it was the very last thing on earth that she wanted him to do. Now that she had found out the identity of her father, though, she knew she wouldn't be able to get back to any sort of normal existence until she had seen him face to face. And to do that, she needed help. *This* man's help, unfortunately.

Anyway, she had already decided that there was no reason why she shouldn't use Lyndon Hyde. She would let him take her to her father, and then dump him. It shouldn't be too difficult. She would simply find some way of shaking him off as soon as she discovered the whereabouts of Malcolm Morgan. Then she would face the meeting with her father on her own. There was definitely no way she was going to allow some journalist to sit in on it, recording every word, so that he could later write about it in a national newspaper!

She raised her head and looked directly into Lyndon's light blue eyes. 'You really know where my father is?'

'Yes,' he replied at once. 'I've a great many contacts. There are a lot of things I can find out without the help of a private detective,' he added, a glimmer of amusement showing on his face for the first time.

Mae didn't smile back at him. 'But you won't tell me where I can find him?'

'I'll take you to him,' he replied.

'That isn't the same thing!'

He shrugged. 'It's the only option that's on offer. Take it or leave it.'

She flung a black look at him. 'You know very well that I've got to take it!'

'Then all we have to do now is to make the arrangements,' he told her, ignoring her outburst of frustrated temper. 'You'll need to take a few days off work, and you'd better pack some clothes suitable for a very warm climate. Cotton skirts and tops, shorts, that kind of thing. You won't need anything very dressy. You do have a passport?'

'Yes.'

'Good. Then be ready early tomorrow morning. I'll pick you up around six.'

'Tomorrow?' Mae repeated a little blankly. She hadn't expected it to be so soon.

'If we don't go straight away, Malcolm Morgan will have moved on. It might be months before we get another chance to see him. If you turn coward at the last moment, I'll simply go on my own. One way or another, I intend to meet up with him face to face.'

She looked at him curiously. 'Why do *you* want to see him so much?'

'I want to get a personal interview with him,' Lyndon said briefly. 'No one's ever managed it before. I intend to make it a first.'

'One way and another, Malcolm Morgan's going to have quite a few new experiences over the next few days!' Mae said rather shakily. Then she got to her feet. 'If we're leaving early in the morning, I suppose I'd better go now. There are quite a lot of things I've got to do.'

'I'll ring for a taxi,' said Lyndon.

'Er—no,' she said hurriedly, remembering her nearly empty purse. 'I'll catch a bus. Or the tube.'

'Short of cash?' he asked at once.

It annoyed her that he could guess the truth so easily.

'Don't offer to pay my fare,' she warned. 'I'm not taking any money from you!'

'It won't be my money,' Lyndon replied, that faint hint of amusement showing in his eyes again now. 'It'll all go down on expenses. So will the trip we're taking tomorrow.'

'I prefer to pay my own way,' Mae said promptly. 'I want you to add up every penny you spend, and when we return to England, you can tell me how much I owe you.'

And she just hoped there would be enough in her meagre savings account to cover the amount! If he chose to travel first class or stay in expensive hotels, then she was going to be in a lot of trouble.

'You're the independent type, aren't you?' he commented. 'Perhaps you take after your father in more ways than you realise.'

'I don't know yet that he *is* my father,' Mae retorted. 'This whole thing could still turn out to be a sick hoax, or a pack of lies that you've invented to give your article an extra edge.'

His blue eyes briefly glinted, as if he didn't at all like her accusation that he'd deliberately invented the whole story. Mae supposed that she had touched on his professional pride. She didn't particularly care, though. The last thing she was going to worry about was hurting this man's feelings!

'Over the next few days, we'll find out if I lied or not,' he said in a level voice. 'And in the meantime, you'd better take this.' He slid a couple of notes from his wallet and handed them to her. When Mae refused to accept them, the corners of his mouth curved into a smile that made her skin suddenly feel as if an army of goose-pimples had just marched over it. 'Look on it as a loan,' he told her. 'The opening of your account with me. And when this is all over, I'll tell you exactly how much you owe me.' His blue gaze slid over her, as if he was beginning to find the combination of red hair and yellow eyes more than a little interesting. 'I'll also let you choose how you want to pay me,' he added softly.

Mae bristled fiercely at the implication behind his words. There was no point in starting an angry slanging match, though. She was going to have to travel to some unknown destination with this man in the morning, and spend quite a lot of time in his company. Although she would try very hard to keep her contact with him down to an absolute minimum!

With deliberate distaste, she took the notes from him, being careful to avoid touching even his fingers.

'I'll borrow this money from you,' she said in an icy tone. 'And I'll pay you back with a cheque. I'll also repay all my other expenses in the same way.'

'That doesn't sound like very much fun,' he murmured.

'I don't expect anything about the next few days to be fun!' Mae shot back at him. 'If you had one iota of sensitivity or understanding, you'd already know that. Journalists are usually a little short on those commodities, though, aren't they?' she went on sarcastically. 'If they weren't, they wouldn't be able to trample all over people's feelings in search of a good story.' She had reached the front door by now, and she pulled it open. 'I'll see you in the morning, Mr Hyde,' she said, keeping her tone cold and distant. 'I don't want to—I don't particularly want to see you ever again—but unfortunately I don't have any option. I just hope that you won't be *too* objectionable over the next few days.'

With that, she slammed the door shut behind her and marched off down the road. And, as she flagged down a taxi, she told herself that she had imagined the dangerous gleam that had lit Lyndon Hyde's eyes as she had delivered that last speech. Because if she hadn't imagined it, she might well be in serious trouble!

* * *

Mae set her alarm clock for five o'clock the next morning, but was awake long before that. In fact, she wasn't sure that she had even been to sleep. She had closed her eyes and tossed and turned for much of the night, but hadn't seemed able to manage even a light doze.

A small suitcase stood in the corner, packed the night before with a selection of light summer clothes. As she crawled out of bed, feeling heavy-eyed and apprehensive, she wondered for the hundredth time if she was doing the right thing. Perhaps it would be better to try and forget everything Lyndon Hyde had told her? Well, not *forget* it, because she knew that would be absolutely impossible, but put it right to the back of her mind and carry on with her normal, humdrum existence? She had managed without a father for twenty-four years. She could easily get through the next twenty-four years—in fact the rest of her life—without him.

Then Mae gave a very heavy sigh. What she *couldn't* do was spend the rest of her life wondering about him. It had been different when she hadn't known who he was. She knew his name now, though, and she could picture the face that went with that name. What she desperately needed to do now was to see him in person. Perhaps then she would finally be able to come to terms with the great gap in her life caused by his abandonment of her.

A glance at her watch told her that she had better not spend any more time brooding over it. Lyndon Hyde would be here very soon, and she had better be ready if she intended to go with him.

After a quick shower, she wriggled into cotton trousers and a loose top. The English summer had been unexpectedly hot and sunny this year, but it was obviously going to be even hotter where they were going. She slid her feet into flat-soled sandals, and then took a quick glance at her reflection. Not exactly elegant, she decided with a small grimace. But at least it was a comfortable outfit for travelling in.

Then she heard a car draw up outside, and her heart gave a sudden heavy thump. She went over to the window and looked nervously out, just in time to see Lyndon getting out of a taxi.

'Well, this is it,' she told herself through gritted teeth. 'You're on your way to see your father!'

A few seconds later, her doorbell rang. Mae picked up her case and a small shoulder-bag which held a few things she might need on the journey. Then she went over to open the door.

It was her first good look at Lyndon this morning— she had only caught a glimpse of him as he had got out of the taxi—and she blinked in surprise.

He looked entirely different. The expensive suit had disappeared. So had the gold watch and cufflinks, and the highly polished shoes. Instead, he was wearing a rather faded pair of jeans and a thin sweatshirt, while on his feet were a distinctly disreputable pair of trainers. Even his dark hair had lost its well-groomed sheen, and looked a little damp and dishevelled, as if he hadn't long stepped out of the shower.

'I take it that this is your holiday outfit?' she said a trifle sarcastically.

'This isn't going to be anything like a holiday,' he warned her. Then he relaxed a little. 'But I do like to be comfortable while I'm travelling,' he went on, with a disarming grin. 'And I don't usually dress as formally as I was yesterday. I had to take a couple of hours off from following you to attend a very formal function, and I didn't bother to change afterwards.' He pointed towards her case. 'Is this all the luggage you've got?'

'I won't need more, will I?' she said with a small frown. 'We are only going to be away a few days, aren't we?'

'If everything goes well, we should be back by the weekend.'

Mae gave a small sigh of relief. She had already had to tell a few lies to explain her absence from work. She had rung them late yesterday and told them she had caught a virus, nothing too serious, but she would be off for the rest of the week. She hadn't at all liked telling those lies, but she hadn't been able to think of any alternative. She had already used up all her holiday allocation, and there was no way they would let her take an extra few days, especially at such short notice. Perhaps if she had explained the circumstances, they might have eventually agreed to give her some sort of compassionate leave, but she hadn't wanted to do that. This was far too private a matter to discuss with people who were comparative strangers. She hadn't even told her friends—or her mother.

She felt distinctly guilty about that. Yet, it was her mother who had imposed this wall of silence where her father was concerned. And she would almost certainly try to stop Mae going ahead with this meeting with the man who was responsible for her existence in this world.

While all these thoughts were running through her head, Lyndon had taken her case from her and was already halfway down the stairs. Then he seemed to realise that she wasn't following him.

'Are you coming?' he demanded, a little impatiently.

'Yes,' she muttered. She took a deep breath, closed the door behind her, and then followed him down the stairs.

Neither of them said a word during the taxi ride to the airport. Mae was beginning to feel slightly disorientated. It was definitely very odd to set off on a journey without knowing where you were going.

Once they reached the airport, Lyndon took charge of all the formalities while she just sat in the lounge, staring at the departure board. As the destinations kept flicking up, she kept wondering which one would be theirs.

Lyndon finally returned, and sat down beside her.

'Our flight leaves in half an hour,' he told her.

'To where?'

He gave a small shrug. 'There's no reason why you shouldn't know. We're going to Athens.'

'That's where my—where Malcolm Morgan is?'

'No. He's on one of the Greek islands. He's taking a short holiday. It's something he does only very rarely, and it's one of the few times—in fact, probably the only time—that he isn't surrounded by members of his staff. This is probably the one chance that we'll get to see him, so try not to blow it.'

'You think I might do that?' she demanded indignantly.

'You might,' Lyndon said in a cool tone. 'Try and remember to be patient. It's no good just charging straight in. We've got to pick the right moment. And above all, do what I tell you at all times. I know a

lot about this man. I know how he thinks and how
he reacts. I can make sure you see him—but only if
you've got sense enough to follow my instructions
exactly.'

Mae sat there and silently fumed. Who did he think
he was, giving her these kind of orders? Anyway,
Malcolm Morgan was *her* father, not his! If she
wanted to walk straight in and see him, then that was
what she would do!

She said none of this to Lyndon, though. There was
no point in arguing about it. Especially as she didn't
even intend that he should be around when she met
Malcolm Morgan for the first time! It was definitely
better to go along with everything he said, for now.
She would pretend to be meek and compliant—if she
could manage it! That way, he wouldn't get too sus-
picious. Then, when the right opportunity came along,
she would slip away from him and lose him.

Mae turned her head slightly, and found that
Lyndon's light blue gaze was resting on her speculatively. She wriggled uncomfortably. She didn't like it
when he looked at her like that. It made her feel as
if he could tell exactly what she was thinking—and
that was a very uncomfortable sensation.

'How do we get to this island?' she said hurriedly,
trying to find some way to distract him.

'From Athens airport, we'll get a bus to the port
of Piraeus. From there, we go by boat.'

'What's the island called?'

'Lindos. It's only a small island, with just a few
private holiday homes on it. Tourists hardly ever go
there, so there isn't a direct ferry service. We'll have
to get a boat to the nearest large island, and then try
and find a local boat to take us to Lindos.'

'I thought someone like Malcolm Morgan would take a holiday somewhere more exotic,' she commented.

'He's a man of surprisingly plain tastes,' Lyndon said. 'Except where women are concerned,' he added drily. 'He's been married three times and had a long string of mistresses—often at the same time. And he seems to go for the exotic type. All of his women have been fairly stunning.'

'Perhaps if he chose them for character and intelligence, instead of just for looks, he'd be more lucky,' Mae retorted.

'Maybe,' Lyndon agreed. 'But, like it or not, it's the physical appearance of someone that ninety-nine per cent of people notice first. It's certainly the first thing that struck me about you,' he went on in a rather huskier tone of voice.

Mae stiffened. It was the first personal remark he had made to her since he had arrived at her flat this morning, and, as far as she was concerned, it could be the last!

'I think looks are highly unimportant,' she stated coldly.

'That's easy to say when you've got a head of dazzling dark red curls, and the kind of eyes that someone could easily remember for the rest of their life,' Lyndon answered disconcertingly. 'But I agree that they're only a very small part of what makes up the complete person. You've no doubt got a lot of other assets that will turn out to be equally memorable. Perhaps I'll discover what some of them are, over the next few days.'

His eyes had taken on an almost sleepy sheen, and Mae found it remarkably hard to tear her own gaze away from them.

'I don't think you'll be discovering anything about me at all,' she muttered fiercely.

Lyndon seemed about to say something, but just at that moment another announcement came over the loudspeakers.

'They're calling our flight,' he told her. 'Let's get moving.'

Mae was more than willing to obey. Anything to put an end to this distinctly odd conversation!

The plane was crowded with cheerful, talkative holiday-makers, but Mae felt very isolated from them. She seemed to be living in a different world; a world full of uncertainties, and with a definite shadow over the immediate future.

She didn't feel like talking, and to her relief Lyndon remained silent. In fact, when she finally turned to look at him, she found that he was asleep.

After her restless night, her own eyes felt pretty heavy, but there was no way she could have slept through the racket going on all around them. Some of the passengers weren't entirely sober, most of the children were over-excited and noisy, and everyone seemed to be talking louder and louder, trying to make themselves heard. She supposed that, if you were going on holiday, it was a great atmosphere. Lyndon had already reminded her that this wouldn't be a holiday for them, though, and she certainly didn't feel in a holiday mood. In fact, she felt increasingly nervous, now that they were actually on their way. She almost wished Lyndon would wake up. It annoyed her to see him so relaxed, when she was so completely on edge!

Lyndon opened his eyes just minutes before the plane was due to touch down at Athens.

'Did you enjoy your sleep?' Mae snapped irritably.

'It helps to pass the time on a tedious journey.'

She scowled at him. 'I'm so sorry that you find my company tedious. I'll try not to bore you too much in the future!'

His mouth remained relaxed, and his blue gaze was calm and steady. 'I didn't mean that, and you know it,' he told her. Then he stretched and yawned. 'Anyway, it was a good chance to catch up on some sleep. I don't seem to have had very much lately.'

'That's because you've spent most of your time following me around,' she retorted waspishly. 'Although I still don't know why you had to do that. What was the point? One good look at me would have told you that I had the same colourings as Malcolm Morgan. And that was all you really wanted to know, wasn't it?'

'Initially—yes. But then I decided that I wanted to find out more about you. And following you around for a couple of days—and nights—was one way of doing that.'

'Why did you want to find out more about me?' Mae demanded. Then she immediately wished that she hadn't asked that question. It might be better not to know the answer.

Lyndon was already replying, though. 'It's always interesting to delve into someone else's life. To know how they spend their time, what they like and dislike, to get inside their head as far as possible and discover what they're thinking and feeling.'

'You couldn't have done all that in just a couple of days!'

'No, I couldn't,' he agreed. 'But I ended up knowing quite a few things about you that you probably wouldn't have told me, if I'd just asked.'

'Such as what?' Mae muttered.

'That you're conscientious, as far as your work's concerned. You arrive on time, don't take a minute longer for lunch than you're allowed, and don't rush off early once you're finished for the day. I knew from the research I'd already done on you that your social life was fairly non-existent. No current boyfriend, and not all that many in the past, either. There was a time when I thought you might not like men.' As Mae bristled at that implication, he gave her a lazy smile. 'As soon as I saw you, though, I dismissed that idea. You like men, all right. But perhaps you don't quite trust them. And why should you, when the most important man in your life abandoned you before you were even born?'

Mae definitely didn't like the way he was dissecting her character. Nor did she like the way he was guessing so accurately!

'Cut the amateur psychology,' she said scornfully. 'And I don't think you've learnt very much about me. Just a few unimportant facts.'

'They're important to me.'

'Why?' she said suspiciously.

'Because it means that I've made a small start towards getting to know you very much better.' Then, before she could think of a suitably dismissive answer, he directed her attention towards the red light above them. 'Fasten your seatbelt,' he instructed her. 'We're coming in to land.'

Mae had known that Greece would be hot at this time of the year, but, even so, she wasn't prepared for the blast of heat that met her as they stepped off the plane at Athens.

Lyndon seemed to know exactly where he was going, and in a remarkably short time he was hustling her on to the bus that would take them to the port of Piraeus. Large numbers of people seemed to be heading in the same direction, and the bus was very full and very hot. They managed to get seats, but Mae found herself squeezed up uncomfortably close to Lyndon, and with no way of wriggling even a couple of inches away from him. He seemed totally unperturbed by the fact that their thighs, hips, upper arms and shoulders were almost moulded together. In fact, Mae had the distinct impression that he was rather enjoying it.

Just take no notice, she told herself firmly. Pretend you're sitting next to a total stranger. You won't have to put up with it for long. This journey can't last forever!

It certainly seemed to go on for a very long time, though. Mae's watch told her that, in reality, it had been less than an hour, but it began to seem more like a day! She spent much of the time staring out of the window, but there wasn't actually very much to see. Anyway, it was difficult to concentrate on anything when all she was actually aware of was the hard pressure of Lyndon's thigh pressing right along the length of her own!

She was thoroughly relieved when the bus finally rattled into Piraeus. It was early afternoon by now, and the sun was hotter than ever. Yet Lyndon still looked infuriatingly cool and unruffled, in complete contrast to the rest of the busload of passengers, with their red and sweating faces.

'Why don't you look as hot as everyone else?' Mae grumbled. 'OK, you don't have to go bright red, but couldn't you at least go a little bit *pink*?'

'The heat never bothers me,' he replied calmly, picking up her suitcase as well as his own bag.

'Then what does bother you?' she demanded irritably.

His light blue eyes gleamed in the bright sunlight. 'Sitting so close to you on that bus,' he said with a lazy grin. 'That needed more self-control that I've exercised for a very long time!'

Mae was sure he was just teasing her. He seemed to enjoy it when she got rattled. Ignore him, she instructed herself, with a small toss of her head which sent her dark red curls dancing.

'Where do we go from here?' she asked in a very cool voice.

'We catch a ferry out to the islands. We'll head for the nearest large island to Lindos, and then we'll probably have to spend the night there. We'll try and get to Lindos first thing tomorrow morning.'

Just the thought of it made Mae shiver nervously, despite the intense heat.

'How long will we be on the ferry?' she asked, trying a little desperately to find something else to think about.

'Five or six hours,' replied Lyndon.

She gave a grimace. This journey seemed to be going on forever!

The ferry turned out to be as packed as the bus from Athens. The Greek islands certainly were a popular destination! she thought to herself wryly, as she trudged aboard. They were going to be packed on to this boat like sardines.

She was determined that there wasn't going to be any repetition of the bus journey, though. She wasn't going to spend the next five or six hours wedged up against Lyndon Hyde!

Mae tapped him firmly on the shoulder. When he turned round to face her, she looked at him with some determination.

'I'd like some time on my own,' she told him. 'There's no reason why we've got to spend the next few hours together. We can go our own way and meet up again when the ferry arrives at its destination.'

To her surprise, he didn't argue with her. Instead, he looked at her thoughtfully for a few seconds. Then he gave a brief nod.

'I suppose you can't get lost or into any trouble on a boat. I'll see you later.'

And, with that, he disappeared into the crowd.

Mae felt an unexpected sense of let-down. She hadn't thought it would be this easy to get away from him for a while. On the other hand, she was glad it hadn't turned into a full-scale confrontation. She really didn't feel up to it right now.

She managed to find a shady place for herself on the deck, preferring to be out in the fresh air rather than crammed into one of the crowded lounges. The sea was fairly calm, for which she was thankful. She dug out a thick paperback she had brought with her, and tried to concentrate on the story.

The ferry stopped at a couple of islands en route, but more people scrambled on to replace those who got off, so it never seemed any less crowded. Mae had long since lost interest in her book. Instead, she stared at the wide blue expanse of the sea—which, rather irritatingly, reminded her of the clear blue of Lyndon's eyes—and occasionally closed her eyes and dozed.

It was early evening by the time the ferry at last chugged into its final port of call. Mae hauled herself to her feet, yawned sleepily a couple of times, and joined the rush of people heading for the shore.

Lyndon was already waiting for her on the quayside. He must have been one of the first off the ferry, Mae thought irritably. In fact, he was probably the type of man who wanted to be first in everything.

As she trudged tiredly over to join him, a dark-haired boy came quickly over and planted himself in front of them.

'You want a room?' he asked. 'I know a good room. Very clean and very cheap.'

'It might be a good idea to take up his offer,' Lyndon said. 'Most of these people getting off the ferry will be looking for rooms. If we don't find somewhere quickly, we might not find anywhere at all.'

Mae was too weary to argue. 'All right,' she agreed. Then her yellow eyes briefly flickered into life again and she turned to the boy. 'We want two rooms,' she said in a very clear voice. 'Do you understand? *Two* rooms.'

The boy looked a little surprised, but then shrugged. 'OK,' he said cheerfully. 'Two rooms. No problem. Come with me.'

He led them through the narrow back streets of the small port, until they finally reached a brightly lit taverna that seemed full to bursting-point with people eating and drinking.

'Do you want some food?' asked the boy.

Mae shook her head. 'I just want to sleep. Where are the rooms?'

He led them up a rickety wooden staircase to a couple of rooms over the taverna. Then he pointed to two doors. 'Two rooms,' he said with a grin. 'You pay now?'

Lyndon peeled off a handful of drachmas and handed them to the boy. He flashed them one last broad smile, and then disappeared down the stairs.

'Which room do you want?' asked Lyndon.

'I don't care,' said Mae, yawning. 'Not as long as it's got a bed.' She pushed open the door nearest to her. 'I'll take this one.'

'Are you sure you don't want to share?' asked Lyndon casually. 'I could always ask for a rebate on the room we don't use.'

She wasn't so tired that she was going to let that pass. 'No, I do not want to share,' she informed him in a very cool voice. 'And if we're going to have to go through this charade every night, then I'd prefer you to find somewhere else to stay.'

'But it's not a charade, as far as I'm concerned.' His voice still sounded lazy and relaxed, but his light blue eyes were bright and alert. 'You don't understand, do you?' he went on, his gaze fixed directly on hers now.

'Understand what?' muttered Mae, wishing he would look away from her. She didn't like being pinned down by that blue gaze.

'I wasn't joking when I said I was having problems with my self-control on the bus,' he told her softly. 'I wasn't even joking when I told you I'd let you choose how you wanted to repay the cost of this trip. And I know exactly what kind of payment I'd like,' he said in a voice that had become positively velvet in texture.

'Well, you won't get it!' she said sharply.

Lyndon merely smiled. 'Maybe. Maybe not. But I'm warning you here and now that I certainly intend to try.'

Her nerve-ends gave a hefty twitch. 'Why?' she demanded angrily.

He shrugged a little resignedly, as if he didn't quite understand it himself. 'I suppose it's because, as soon as I saw you, I knew that you were someone I really wanted, Mae Stanfield,' he replied at last. Then he opened the door to his own room. 'Sleep well,' he said.

Mae scowled edgily at his door as he closed it behind him. She wished the wretched man would disappear right off the face of the earth. Then she might—just *might*—be able to get a decent night's sleep!

CHAPTER THREE

MAE'S bed turned out to be far from comfortable, with a hard mattress and a small, thin pillow. On top of that, the noise drifting up from the taverna below seemed to go on until well into the early hours of the morning. Every time she closed her eyes, a loud burst of laughter or good-natured shouting made her open them again and thump her pillow in frustration. Then, just when she finally started to slip into a light doze, someone started singing!

She told herself that it was definitely all this disturbance that was keeping her awake. It didn't have anything at all to do with those last remarks Lyndon had made to her.

Anyway, he hadn't meant them, Mae assured herself for the dozenth time. He had been winding her up, that was all. He seemed to get a kick out of doing that. Or perhaps he was just getting his own back because she had wanted to be by herself on that long ferry trip. His male pride had been dented. Men like Lyndon Hyde couldn't believe it when a woman told them that they didn't want them around!

The noise from the taverna finally began to die down, and she gave a sigh of relief. Perhaps now she could get some sleep! She closed her eyes, made an effort to relax her tense body, but still stayed awake.

Oh, this was impossible! she told herself, sitting up and glaring into the darkness.

She got out of bed and padded over to the window. There was a huge moon in the sky, but it was surprisingly chilly after the intense heat of the day. She rubbed her bare arms, and was about to go back to bed and dive under the thin blanket when she saw Lyndon walking along the road below.

The moon gave off enough bright, silvery light for her to see him quite clearly. He was striding along fairly quickly, and she had the feeling that he had been out for some time.

Her own room was in darkness and she had drawn back slightly from the window when she had first seen him, so she was quite sure that he wouldn't notice her standing there. A few yards further on, though, he suddenly came to an abrupt halt, lifted his head, and stared straight up at her.

Mae immediately backed even further away from the window. For some reason, she didn't want him to see her looking down at him.

He stood there in the middle of the street for a few moments. Then he slowly began to walk forward again, heading towards the taverna.

She tiptoed silently over to the door, and held her breath as she heard him coming up the stairs. He seemed to halt for a moment when he reached the top, and Mae's heart gave an extra heavy thump. Then his door opened and closed, and there was nothing except silence.

A little shakily, she went back to her own bed and flopped on to it.

He couldn't sleep, so he went for a walk, she told herself. It's got nothing to do with you, though. You're not the reason for his insomnia. Just as *he's* got nothing to do with the reason why *you* can't sleep tonight.

She closed her eyes very firmly and, eventually, managed to snatch a couple of hours of restless sleep.

When she woke up again, the sun was glaring through the window of the sparsely furnished, but clean, room. She rubbed her eyes, which seemed to have felt permanently heavy and aching during the last couple of days, and then forced herself out of bed.

She found a small bathroom just along from her room, although the facilities were fairly limited, with little more than a trickle of tepid water coming out of the tap. Mae washed as best she could, and then pulled on a thin cotton skirt and matching top. It was already very hot, even though it was still quite early, and she guessed the sun would be blazing down with a quite savage heat by midday.

When she finally went downstairs, she found Lyndon sitting at a table in one corner of the taverna. It had been laid with a clean tablecloth and cutlery, and he pointed to the chair opposite him as she came in.

'Sit down and have something to eat. The boy's mother has agreed to provide us with breakfast.'

Mae didn't feel in the least hungry, but it seemed ages since she had last had a decent meal, so she supposed she ought to make an effort to eat something.

'Couldn't you sleep last night?' Lyndon went on casually.

She jumped quite visibly. So, he *had* seen her.

'I—er—just woke up for a few minutes,' she said hurriedly.

The gleam in his eyes told her that he didn't believe her, but to her relief he didn't say anything more on the subject.

The food, when it came, was simple but well-cooked, and Mae managed to eat her way through quite a large amount of it, despite the fact that Lyndon's blue gaze kept fixing on her far more often than she would have liked. They finished the meal with a couple of cups of sweet, strong coffee, which helped to chase the heaviness from her eyes and the leaden tiredness from her limbs.

As soon as they had finished, Lyndon stood up. 'We'd better go and see if we can find a boat to take us to Lindos,' he said without preamble.

Mae immediately began to feel very nervous inside. There had been times during the night when she had almost forgotten why they were here. She began to remember it now with great clarity, though. And she wasn't at all sure that she was ready for the coming confrontation with the man who could very well turn out to be her father.

Lyndon was already striding towards the door, though, and after a few moments' hesitation she began to trot along after him.

As they left the taverna, the dark-haired boy who had brought them there suddenly appeared in front of them.

'Kalimera,' he greeted them. 'Would you like me to show you around the island? I'm a good guide. Very cheap.'

'Thanks for the offer, but we're not staying on this island,' Lyndon told him. 'We're going to Lindos.'

The boy looked puzzled. 'Why do you want to go there? There is nothing at Lindos, no tavernas, no discos, no shops, nothing to do. Why not stay on this island? You will like it here much better. And if you take your rooms for a whole week, you can have them at a special price.'

'That's a very generous offer,' said Lyndon, suppressing a grin, 'but I'm afraid we still want to go to Lindos.'

The boy shrugged philosophically. 'Then my cousin will probably take you. He is delivering supplies to the island this morning. And he will not charge you too much.'

'Where can we find your cousin?' asked Lyndon.

'He will be at the quayside,' replied the boy. 'Come, I will take you to him.'

The boy shot off, with Lyndon walking fairly quickly behind him, but Mae followed them much more slowly. She hadn't thought it would be quite this easy to get to Lindos. In fact, she had been expecting to have to wait a day—or perhaps even two—before finding a boat to take them there. They weren't going to have to wait any time at all, though. They were setting off this morning, and just the thought of it made her stomach churn.

When she reached the quayside, she found Lyndon in conversation with a tall, swarthy man, with the boy acting as interpreter. A couple of minutes later, money changed hands. Then Lyndon turned, saw her, and gestured to her to come over.

'We're in luck,' he said. 'This is the boy's cousin, and he's leaving for Lindos right now. We've just got time to go back to the taverna and collect our things.'

Mae swallowed hard. 'Do we—do we have to go on *this* boat?' she asked in a small voice.

'Yes, we do,' Lyndon replied at once. 'It might be days before we can find another boat going to the island. Tourists hardly ever bother to visit it, so boats go there only infrequently, to deliver supplies to people who have holiday homes there.'

Mae just didn't feel ready for this, though. It was only a couple of days since Lyndon had barged into her life, with his startling information about her father, and ever since then she seemed to have been rushed into one decision after another, each one a little harder to make than the last. Now she was in the Greek islands, and perhaps only an hour or so away from coming face to face with Malcolm Morgan, who might or might not be her father, and she needed more *time*. She didn't even have the slightest idea what she was going to say to him. 'Hello, Dad,' seemed a bit premature! And what if it turned out that he *wasn't* her father? She needed to prepare herself for that possibility, as well.

'I don't think——' she croaked. Then she cleared her throat and said more clearly, 'I don't think I want to go on this boat. It doesn't—doesn't look at all seaworthy,' she finished rather feebly, determined not to admit to Lyndon her real reasons for not wanting to get on board.

Lyndon's blue gaze looked directly at her. 'Do you want to see Malcolm Morgan, or not?' he challenged her.

'Well—yes,' she said, although without a great deal of conviction.

His eyes narrowed. 'You've changed your mind? Or are you just turning coward, now that it's nearly time to meet him face to face?'

Since Mae was never in a million years going to admit to this man that she was scared of anything, she drew herself up to her full height and glared at him. 'I'm not a coward!' she lied to him furiously. 'And if this old tub is the only thing that can take us to Lindos, then I suppose we'd better get on board. I just hope it doesn't sink before it gets there!'

She clambered on to the boat and then sat cross-legged on the hard deck, still glaring at Lyndon.

'What about your luggage?' he reminded her. 'It's still at the taverna.'

'If you were a gentleman, you'd offer to collect it for me.'

'I think that I must be a gentleman, or I'd have made more of an effort to get into your room last night.'

That remark really grated on her already raw nerves. 'A gentleman wouldn't have tried to get in my room at all!' Mae snapped at him.

His blue eyes radiated lazy amusement. 'Only someone who was totally impotent wouldn't have made any effort. And believe me, I don't fall into that category.'

Mae believed him! She also thought it was definitely time this particular conversation came to an end.

'I don't think we should discuss this any further,' she said coldly. She gestured towards the tall Greek who owned the boat. 'I'm sure he doesn't want to listen to this type of conversation. In fact, you're probably making him feel very embarrassed.'

'I'm not embarrassing him at all,' Lyndon said calmly.

'How do you know that?' she demanded.

'Because he hasn't understood a word either of us have said. He doesn't speak English.'

Mae scowled. 'When I'm with you, there are times when I wish *I* didn't speak English!' When he still stood there, grinning at her in that peculiarly irritating way, her scowl deepened. 'Oh, why don't you go and get the luggage?' she said irritably.

To her surprise, Lyndon nodded in cheerful agreement. Then he swung round and set off in the direction of the taverna.

Once he was out of sight, it suddenly occurred to Mae that this might be the very chance she had been waiting for. If she could just persuade the owner of this boat to leave right now, leaving Lyndon behind, she would have achieved one of her major objectives on this trip. She could make the journey to Lindos on her own, and have her first meeting with Malcolm Morgan without having Lyndon standing a couple of feet behind, listening to everything they said to each other—and, worse than that, writing about it in his feature article!

The dark-haired boy was still standing on the quayside. Mae called to him, and he came hurrying over.

'Listen,' she said a little breathlessly, 'I want you to tell your cousin to leave straight away. Will you do that?'

The boy looked puzzled. 'But your gentleman friend—he isn't back yet.'

'He isn't my friend. And he certainly isn't a gentleman! Look,' she said with some urgency, 'talk to your cousin. Please! Tell him that I want to leave *now*.'

The boy gave a baffled shrug, but to Mae's relief he then began to talk rapidly to the tall man. A fairly lengthy exchange followed, and when it was finally over the boy turned back to Mae.

'My cousin says he cannot leave yet.'

'Why?' demanded Mae.

'Because the gentleman isn't here.'

She gave an exasperated sigh. 'But that's the whole point. I want to leave without him.'

'My cousin understands that, but he says that it was the gentleman who paid for the boat. Therefore he will not leave without him.'

Mae felt like kicking something in frustration. Even here, in the Greek islands, men still stuck together!

'*I'll* pay your cousin,' she said in a last frantic attempt to get her own way. 'I'll pay him double! Tell him that.'

The boy translated Mae's offer, and this time the tall Greek turned to look at Mae thoughtfully. The offer of more money seemed to be having some effect.

'Three times as much,' said Mae recklessly. 'But he must leave immediately.'

She glanced anxiously at the road leading from the quayside. It wouldn't take Lyndon very long to fetch their luggage from the taverna. Unless she could clinch this deal right now, it was going to be too late.

There was one more brief exchange between the boy and his cousin. 'All right,' said the boy, to Mae's intense relief. 'But you must pay him now, in advance.'

Mae began to scrabble for her bag, but then suddenly stopped. She didn't have any Greek money! How could she, when she hadn't even known where they were going until they had reached the airport?

And so far she hadn't needed any, because Lyndon had paid for everything.

She looked at the boy forlornly. 'I suppose he won't take a credit card?'

The boy didn't even bother to translate her offer. 'Cash,' he said firmly.

She sighed. 'Then you'd better tell him the deal's off.'

The tall Greek looked highly displeased as the boy passed on this last piece of information. Her only consolation was that he couldn't tell Lyndon about any of this, since he didn't speak English.

She stared gloomily down at the deck and wondered if anything was *ever* going to go right for her. Once Lyndon was actually on Lindos with her, it was going to be very much harder to get rid of him. In fact, she couldn't see how she was going to manage it at all.

Almost as if thinking about him had magically conjured him up, she heard his voice behind her.

'Ready to leave?'

He had jumped on board, and was just dumping their luggage in the front of the boat.

'I suppose so,' she said without much enthusiasm.

Lyndon nodded at the tall Greek, who disappeared below. A couple of minutes later, an asthmatic-sounding engine coughed reluctantly into life. The dark-haired boy untied the mooring ropes and tossed them on board. Then he stood on the quayside and waved cheerfully at them as the boat chugged slowly out to sea.

'How long is this trip going to take?' asked Mae.

'About half an hour, I should think,' replied Lyndon, settling himself comfortably on the deck beside her. 'Lindos isn't all that far. Look over there,' he said, pointing to his left. 'You can actually see it on the horizon.'

It was little more than a small dark blob in the distance, but just looking at it made Mae feel rather funny inside. Malcolm Morgan was there. And he was going to be very surprised—and probably not in the least pleased—to see her.

The boat chugged on across the water, which was quite calm again today. Mae knew that they had been lucky with the weather. Strong winds often blew in the Cyclades during the summer months, and the sea sometimes became too rough for the smaller boats to negotiate.

Lindos gradually loomed nearer and took shape. It was a small island, with a rocky shoreline and dusty brown hills dotted with small patches of green. Not particularly beautiful, but definitely secluded. The kind of place to come if you wanted to be alone. Or if you were the type of man who led a very full and public life, so that a few days of privacy now and then were absolutely essential.

The boat began to approach a tiny natural harbour. There was a small quayside and a couple of houses, but that was it. No tavernas, no shops, no hotels— nothing! Just a handful of people waiting for the boat, ready to collect their supplies.

Mae found herself swallowing hard as the boat got near enough to make out their faces. What if Malcolm Morgan had come down in person to pick up his supplies?

Of the half a dozen men standing there, though, none had dark red hair. She began to breathe a little more easily. She wasn't going to have to face that particular confrontation just yet.

'Well, this is Lindos,' remarked Lyndon, coming over to stand beside her as the boat began to maneouvre towards the quayside. 'What do you think of it?'

'It's probably very nice, if you like Greek islands. Right now, though, I'd like to be a thousand miles away from here,' she said fervently. Then she was immediately annoyed with herself. She had never meant to admit how very nervous it made her just to be here.

'Don't worry,' said Lyndon calmly. 'I'm here, if you need any help.'

'Oh, that's very comforting!'

His eyes flickered briefly, as if her response hadn't at all pleased him. Mae didn't really care, though. And she was quite certain that, if she needed help, the very last person she would turn to would be Lyndon Hyde!

The boat was alongside the small quay now. The engines had been cut, and the mooring ropes were being secured. A couple of minutes later, the people who had been standing on the quayside were swarming aboard, helping to unload the supplies. They were shouting cheerfully to each other, but none of them seemed to speak a word of English.

'Where do we go from here?' asked Mae, looking around.

'To Malcolm Morgan's villa,' Lyndon replied.

His reply sent a small shiver right through her. To try and disguise it, she tossed her dark red curls and looked very sceptical. 'And how do we find it?' she enquired. 'It'll be rather hard to ask someone where it is, unless we resort to sign-language. There's a definite communication problem around here!'

'We don't need to ask anyone. We simply wait and see who comes to collect those boxes over there.' He pointed to half a dozen small crates that were standing slightly to one side on the quay. 'The ones marked "Malcolm Morgan, Aghios Nikolaos".'

Mae stared at the boxes. She hadn't noticed them before.

'Do you—do you think he'll come and pick them up himself?' she asked in a voice that was beginning to show an annoying tendency to quaver.

'I shouldn't think so,' said Lyndon, to her relief. She didn't think this quayside would be an ideal place for her first meeting with Malcolm Morgan. Now that she thought about it, though, she couldn't think where *would* be a good place.

'You mean, he'll send someone to collect them?' she said. 'But what do we do then?'

'We see which direction they set off in. And then we follow.'

'On foot?' said Mae, her eyebrows shooting up. 'We'll lose them in about half a minute!'

'It doesn't matter,' replied Lyndon. 'The island isn't very big. As soon as we know which direction to head in, it shouldn't take us too long to find Aghios Nikolaos.'

'That's the name of Malcolm Morgan's villa?'

Lyndon nodded. 'St Nicholas. Not very appropriate,' he commented. 'From what I've learned of Malcolm Morgan, the man's a very long way from being a saint!'

Mae had the feeling that could equally well apply to Lyndon Hyde. She didn't intend to tell him that to his face, though. She had enough problems to cope with, at the moment!

The rest of the supplies had been unloaded from the boat now, and were being hauled away in Jeeps, trucks, and even a donkey and cart. Soon, Mae and Lyndon were the only two people left on the quayside.

The tall Greek who had brought them to Lindos untied the mooring ropes on his boat, and started up the engine. He flashed them a dazzling smile, waved, and then began to head his boat out to sea.

'When's he coming back to collect us?' asked Mae, sudden panic beginning to roll over her as the boat got smaller and smaller. 'I don't want to stay on this island for too long. In fact, I want to be off of here by this evening. I can see my—I can see Malcolm Morgan this afternoon,' she amended hurriedly. She couldn't quite bring herself to say 'my father', not at this particular moment. 'Then, afterwards, I want to leave straight away.'

'You don't think it might take a little longer than one afternoon to get things straightened out between you?' Lyndon commented.

'I don't know how long it's going to take. It might even turn out that he *isn't* my father, even though you keep insisting that he is. Either way, I don't want to stay here for more than a few hours. Not on this first visit.'

'Malcolm Morgan is your father,' Lyndon said in a rather different tone of voice. 'Believe that, even if you don't believe anything else I tell you. And as for getting off this island before nightfall—that might not be too easy.'

Mae stared at him suspiciously. 'What do you mean?'

'Boats only call here infrequently. I told you that,' he reminded her. 'It might be a couple of days before there's a boat that can take us off.'

'Are you telling me that the boat that brought us here isn't coming back to collect us?' she demanded.

'Of course it isn't. It's going on to deliver supplies to other islands. We paid for a one-way trip.'

'You didn't tell me that!' she howled at him.

'You didn't ask,' he pointed out with infuriating calmness.

'But we can't stay here!'

'Why not?'

'For a start, there aren't any hotels,' Mae reminded him hotly.

'We can sleep rough, if we have to,' Lyndon replied easily. 'I've done it before.'

'Well, I haven't. And I don't intend to start now.'

His dark eyebrows lifted. 'Where's your sense of adventure?'

'I haven't got one,' Mae retorted. Then she stared frustratedly out to sea. 'There must be some way to get off this island,' she muttered.

'Not unless you're a *very* good swimmer.' Then the smile that had been lurking at the corners of his mouth suddenly disappeared, and a sharp alertness lit his light blue eyes. 'It looks as if someone's finally coming to pick up Malcolm Morgan's supplies,' he commented softly.

Mae turned round, and saw a Jeep bumping its way towards the quayside. Immediately, her mouth and throat went bone-dry, and she felt light-headed. What if Malcolm Morgan himself got out of that Jeep? What would she do? What would she say to him?

The Jeep trundled to a halt and Mae almost stopped breathing. Then the door opened and a man got out.

His hair was grey, not dark red, and he was short and a little overweight instead of powerfully built. Mae felt her racing pulses gradually begin to return to a more normal tempo, and she let out the pent-up breath she had been holding.

At the same time, she became aware that Lyndon's hand was lightly gripping her arm.

'Why are you holding on to me?' she demanded.

'You looked as if you could do with some physical support,' he answered easily. 'I've never seen anyone go quite so white, so very quickly.'

'I'm fair-skinned,' Mae shot back at once. 'I've never got very much colour. And, since I'm perfectly all right, you can let go of me!'

He released her arm immediately, although she thought she saw a flicker of regret in his eyes.

Mae rubbed her skin, as if trying to erase the memory of his touch.

'So, what do we do now?' she muttered.

'We stand around and try to look like tourists,' Lyndon replied. 'We don't want to arouse any suspicions.'

The grey-haired man was beginning to load the boxes of supplies into the Jeep. He threw a couple of half-curious glances in their direction, but apart from that didn't take any notice of them. When the last box had been chucked into the back, he climbed back into the Jeep and drove off.

Lyndon immediately slung his bag over his shoulder. 'Let's start walking,' he said.

'What are we going to do?' she said with a scowl. 'Follow that Jeep?'

'Yes,' he said simply. Then he set off at a brisk pace, leaving Mae with the option of following him, or staying on the quayside all on her own.

It wasn't much of a choice! she decided with an even darker scowl. Although she wished that she *could* stay here. It would be stupid to come so far, though, and not take the last few steps that would take her to Aghios Nikolaos—and Malcolm Morgan.

She picked up her own case and began to trudge off after Lyndon.

The Jeep had disappeared along a narrow, dusty track that led off round the low hill that loomed up behind the small harbour. Lyndon strode quickly and easily in the same direction, and Mae almost had to run at times to keep up with him. She was soon hot and sweaty, as the sun poured down on them, and she was dying for a long, cool drink.

'What if we can't find the villa?' she said, trying not to pant too hard because Lyndon wasn't even breathing faster than normal, and she didn't want him to think that she was totally unfit.

'We'll find it,' he said confidently.

'You always think everything's going to turn out right for you,' she grumbled.

'Have we hit any problems yet?'

'I suppose not,' Mae conceded reluctantly.

'Then trust me. I'll get you through this.'

Mae was sure that no woman in her right mind would ever trust Lyndon Hyde! Not if she had a single ounce of sense.

The road began to wind more steeply up the hill, and by the time they were near the top Mae was way past the point where she could pretend she wasn't out of breath. She was openly puffing, and making a mental reservation to join a keep-fit class as soon as she got back to England.

'Want to rest for a couple of minutes?' asked Lyndon.

'It's only the heat,' she insisted. 'I'd be perfectly all right if it weren't so hot.'

He didn't say anything. He simply raised one eyebrow rather sceptically, which made her so annoyed that she turned her back on him.

Lyndon waited until she had got her breath back. Then he picked up his bag again. 'We'd better start moving,' he said.

Mae suddenly rounded on him. 'Why are you doing this?' she demanded.

His dark brows began to draw together. 'Why?' he repeated. 'I'd have thought that was perfectly obvious. I'm taking you to your father.' His blue eyes narrowed. 'You do want to see him, don't you?'

'I don't know,' she muttered. 'Sometimes I think that I do. But sometimes I think that you've talked me into this whole thing. And I definitely don't know why you're so determined to make me go through with this meeting with Malcolm Morgan.'

Lyndon stared hard at her. For a few moments, she thought he wasn't going to answer her. Then he gave a low growl, and threw down his bag again.

'Why am I doing this?' he said, in a tone that was completely different from any she had ever heard him use before. 'Because we're very alike, you and me, Mae. We share a lot of things. We share the same kind of background.'

'We don't share anything at all,' she retorted. 'As far as I can see, we've got absolutely nothing in common!'

'How about the lack of a parent? Or, in my case, the lack of both?'

His terse questions caught her off balance. She stared at him warily.

'What are you talking about?'

'I was dumped on the doorstep of a hospital when I was just a few hours old,' Lyndon said evenly. 'I don't know who my mother was, or my father, and there's no way I can ever find out. You did rather better than me. You've at least got a mother, and now you've got a chance to find your father.' He looked straight into her shocked eyes, his own light blue gaze now blazingly bright. 'I know exactly what it's like to be without a parent. What a great gap it leaves in your life, all the nights you lie awake wondering about them, all the daydreams you have about one day finding them. Well, it's not a daydream any more, Mae. You're going to have the chance to do what I'm *never* going to be able to do—meet the man who was responsible for your birth. And I'm going to make sure you don't throw away that opportunity through sheer cowardice!'

CHAPTER FOUR

MAE couldn't say a single word for a very long time. And, by the time she did finally find her voice, Lyndon had swung away from her and begun to stride off up the road.

She had to run to catch up with him. When she eventually reached him, rather breathless by now, he shot a fierce look at her.

'I don't want to discuss what I just told you,' he warned in a grim voice. 'I never meant to say as much as I did. Just forget it.'

Mae stared at him in pure disbelief. '*Forget* it? How on earth am I meant to do that?'

Lyndon came to an abrupt halt. 'Look,' he said tersely, 'it's very personal, it's very private, and I don't intend to talk about it any further. Get it?'

'Oh, yes, I get it,' Mae retorted. 'It's all right for you to interfere in *my* life and pry into all my private affairs, but *I'm* not allowed to do the same. Well, that doesn't seem very fair to me!'

His mouth set into a thin smile that held absolutely no trace of any amusement. 'Whoever said that life was fair?'

Mae glared at him. 'You seem to be doing all right.'

'Yes, I'm doing all right,' he agreed. 'So let's just leave the entire subject, shall we?'

But Mae wasn't ready yet to do that. 'You can't throw something like that at me and then pretend it isn't important!'

Lyndon's eyes suddenly took on a new light. 'I didn't say it wasn't important. Only that I don't intend to discuss it.'

'Why?' demanded Mae.

'Because I don't want to,' he replied, with a note of such finality in his voice that she was finally forced to accept that she wasn't going to get any more information out of him. Not right now, anyway. Of course, that didn't mean that she wouldn't try again later on.

He began to walk off at some speed again. Mae trudged along behind him, more slowly this time, and reflected that the past couple of days had held more surprises than she felt capable of handling! What else was Lyndon going to spring on her before this trip was over?

She realised that this revelation about his own lack of parents was just about the first personal fact she had found out about him. Oh, she knew a little about his background, of course. She had already discovered that he drove an extremely expensive car, lived in a very up-market part of London, and worked as a journalist. That was about it, though. And even those few facts didn't add up. She didn't know what journalists earned, but even if he was at the very top of his profession—and Mae had the feeling that Lyndon Hyde would always be at the top of anything he attempted—he surely wouldn't earn enough to support that kind of lifestyle? None of it seemed to make any sense.

And he obviously wasn't going to enlighten her about any of it. At least, not yet.

Lyndon had reached the brow of the hill now, and Mae saw that he was waiting for her to catch up with him. She stared at him as she puffed her way up those last few yards, and almost felt as if she were seeing him for the very first time.

The sun was shining directly on him, illuminating him with startling clarity. A tall man, who seemed as much at ease in faded jeans and a thin sweatshirt as he had been in the very formal clothes he had been wearing when Mae had first come face to face with him. His hair was tousled and gleamed darkly, so that the light blue blaze of his eyes stood out in startling contrast. His skin obviously tanned easily because it was already taking on a golden glow. He seemed very relaxed, despite the tension there had been between them only minutes ago, but Mae wasn't fooled. She was sure the relaxation was only a façade. This man was driven by complex motives and emotions that she hadn't even begun to understand yet.

A few seconds later, she caught up with him. As she stood alongside him, she felt uncharacteristically lost for words. Then her gaze slid past him and fixed on the view that now stretched out in front of them. Her eyes opened much wider, and for a few moments she almost forgot about Lyndon Hyde and all the problems he was causing her.

The scenery had suddenly and dramatically improved. They were looking down on a small bay, the sea a startlingly bright blue as it reflected the sky. Instead of being dusty brown and rather bare, the hillsides were covered with trees. Olive trees sprawled untidily, the branches of lemon and orange trees already gleamed with fruit, while tall dark cypresses loomed in the background. And tucked into the side of the cliffs that ringed the bay was a white-walled villa, washed with sunshine. It had windows and terraces facing out to sea, and great tubs overflowing with flowers to soften the severity of its lines.

'It looks as if we've found Malcolm Morgan's holiday home,' Lyndon said softly.

'What do we do now?' she asked in a voice that had begun to croak nervously.

'We go and knock at the front door,' he replied calmly.

'Er—couldn't we wait for a little while?'

Lyndon's blue eyes looked at her directly. 'How long do you want to wait? An hour? A day? A couple of weeks? Indefinitely?'

Mae swallowed hard. 'I just don't feel—quite ready for this,' she admitted in a low tone.

'You could wait forever, and you still wouldn't feel ready,' Lyndon said evenly. 'In fact, the longer you leave it, the worse it will be. You might as well do it right now, and get it over with.'

She bit her lip 'All right,' she muttered at last.

When he began to move off in the direction of the villa, though, she still dawdled behind. Realising that she wasn't following him, he came back and caught hold of her wrist.

'Come on,' he said firmly, and he began to tow her along.

'I don't need to be dragged there!' she said indignantly.

'I think that you do.' His fingers locked more tightly around her. With a rising sense of panic, she realised that he didn't intend to let go of her until they were standing at the door to Malcolm Morgan's villa. He was going to force her to go through with this, even if she decided at the last minute that she didn't want to, and tried to run away.

After a couple of futile efforts to struggle free, she glared at him.

'You're a very overbearing man!'

'And you're a coward, Mae Stanfield. I've virtually had to drag you every step of the way on this journey. If I hadn't stayed close to you, you'd have run off long before this.'

'I would not!' she denied hotly. 'I could have made it on my own. I *would* have made it. I didn't need you, not for one single second.'

Lyndon abruptly released her wrist. 'Then take these last few steps on your own,' he challenged her softly. 'Walk up to that door and knock on it. Do it all by yourself.'

'I will!' she said, her yellow eyes flashing brightly.

She walked ahead quickly and purposefully, tossing back her dark red curls in a defiant gesture. She could run her life without any help from Lyndon Alexander Hyde! And he was about to find out that she definitely wasn't the coward that he had more than once accused her of being.

Mae actually got as far as the entrance to the villa before her legs started to falter. Up close, it was larger and more imposing than it had looked from a distance. It was built right into the hillside so that it blended effortlessly into the landscape. The sun reflected with dazzling brilliance off the white walls as she looked up at it, and when she looked down she could see a series of steps leading to the blue waters of the bay below.

Well, this was it, she told herself in a shaky voice. All she had to do now was to walk through that open archway, knock on the door that lay beyond, and she

would finally be face to face with Malcolm Morgan—
who might, or might not, be her father.

Except that she couldn't do it. A fierce anger at
Lyndon had got her this far, but somehow it wasn't
quite enough to get her any further. Lyndon was right,
she admitted to herself with a gulp. She *was* a coward.
She just wasn't going to be able to go through this by
herself.

Almost as if he had read her thoughts, Lyndon appeared at her side. His hand slipped under her arm,
his fingers warm against her skin. He didn't say anything; he simply pushed her forward gently but firmly.
And it was funny, but now that he was here she found
she could take those last few steps.

They walked side by side under the archway, and
it was Lyndon who knocked at the door, as if he knew
that her nerveless fingers just didn't have the strength.
His other hand still propped her up, and she was
grateful for that, because her legs were beginning to
feel like unset jelly.

The door opened very quickly. Mae hardly had time
to catch her breath. Then she slowly breathed out
again as she saw a middle-aged woman standing there,
looking at them with a pleasant smile.

'Are you lost?' she asked. 'Do you need directions?'

'No,' replied Lyndon. 'We'd like to see Malcolm
Morgan. This is his villa, isn't it?'

The woman looked rather puzzled. 'Yes, it is. But
he didn't tell me that he was expecting visitors.'

Mae somehow found her voice. 'He—he isn't
expecting us. But we'd like to see him, if it's possible.'

'I'm afraid that it isn't,' replied the woman.

Lyndon's voice became much less affable. 'We've come a long way. I think that the least he could do is spare us a few minutes of his time.'

'Oh, it isn't that he won't see you,' the woman said quickly. 'It's just that he isn't here.'

'Not here?' echoed Mae, in a flat tone. She couldn't quite believe it. She had been through all this hassle and emotional turmoil, and he wasn't even at the villa!

'I'm Mrs Matthews,' the woman said, as if suddenly realising that she hadn't introduced herself. 'I'm Mr Morgan's housekeeper. Can I help you in any way?'

'I'm afraid not,' Lyndon said evenly. 'I'm Lyndon Hyde, by the way, and this is Mae Stanfield. We're here to talk to Mr Morgan about a very private matter.'

'Are you on holiday in the islands?' asked Mrs Matthews.

'No,' said Mae. 'We've come all the way from England, just to see Mr Morgan.'

'Then it must be about something very important,' said the housekeeper. 'Do you want to leave a message with me? I can pass it on to him as soon as he returns.'

'Then he is coming back here, to the villa?' said Lyndon.

'Oh, yes. Probably not until the weekend, though. He's gone off in his yacht for a few days, cruising around the islands.'

Mae looked at Lyndon with a rather dismayed expression. They hadn't counted on anything like this. What were they going to do now?

'Is there anywhere on the island we can stay?' asked Lyndon.

Mrs Matthews shook her head. 'I'm afraid not. There are only private holiday homes, like this one.'

She looked at Lyndon, and then at Mae. 'You're going to stay on Lindos, until Mr Morgan returns?'

'Miss Stanfield has to see him,' Lyndon said firmly.

Mrs Matthews looked at Mae. 'Do you know Mr Morgan?'

Lyndon answered for her. 'Yes, in a way she knows him.'

The housekeeper continued to look at both of them for some time. Then she seemed to make her mind up about something.

'There are plenty of empty rooms in the villa,' she said. 'Would you like to stay here, until Mr Morgan comes back again?'

Mae blinked in surprise. She had never expected the housekeeper to make them an offer like that. Lyndon was already smiling at Mrs Matthews, though, the kind of smile that would have charmed any female from eight to eighty.

'That's very kind of you. We'd certainly like to take up your offer, if you're sure it's not too much trouble.'

Mae stared at him in disbelief. Why was he saying that? We can't stay here, she wanted to scream at him. Not here! But Lyndon wasn't even looking at her.

'It won't be any trouble,' Mrs Matthews was saying comfortably. 'Normally, Mr Morgan wouldn't agree to two strangers staying here, of course. He likes peace and privacy when he has a few days' holiday. But since you've come all the way from England especially to see him, I don't suppose he'll mind. And there isn't anywhere else on the island you can stay. There isn't even a boat that'll take you back to one of the main islands.'

'We thought we might have to sleep rough,' Lyndon said, with another dazzlingly charming smile. 'But Miss Stanfield didn't like that idea very much.'

'I was only joking,' Mae said quickly. 'I don't mind sleeping rough at all. And we can't possibly stay here. We can't expect Mrs Matthews to take in two perfect strangers.' She flashed a pleading look at Lyndon, willing him to look back at her and understand the message she was frantically sending him. His blue gaze seemed to be deliberately avoiding hers, though.

'It's no problem,' Mrs Matthews assured her. 'The villa has a small, self-contained apartment, which you can use. Mr Morgan often allows friends of his to stay there. I'm sure he won't mind if you use it for a couple of days, until he returns.'

Mae was quite certain that he would object—and most strongly!—when he discovered the identity of his uninvited guests. Lyndon was already picking up their luggage, though, thanking Mrs Matthews, and walking into the villa.

Mae's own legs refused to move. She stood outside the doorway, absolutely rooted to the spot. Unlike Lyndon, she just wasn't capable of calmly strolling into Malcolm Morgan's house.

Lyndon finally seemed to realise that she wasn't following him. He returned to the doorway, caught hold of her arm, and yanked her inside.

'I don't want to set foot in this house!' she hissed at him under her breath.

'Why not?' he said softly. 'You're perfectly entitled to be here. In fact, if you'd had a normal childhood, with a father who was willing to admit your existence, you'd probably have spent quite a lot of time here.'

She had never thought of looking at it in that way before. Lyndon was right, though. If Malcolm Morgan *was* her father, then this house was her home.

With that novel thought still whirling round inside her head, she trailed along behind Lyndon and Mrs Matthews as they made their way through the villa. She began to look at the rooms they passed through with fresh curiosity. They were furnished with unexpected simplicity, with tiled floors and pale, colour-washed walls giving an impression of coolness. The furniture was functional and comfortable, with brightly patterned cushions and rugs to give warm splashes of colour.

They reached the far end of the villa, and Mrs Matthews opened a door. 'This is the apartment,' she said. 'As I told you, it's quite self-contained. The freezer's full of food—Mr Morgan likes to keep it well-stocked, in case guests turn up unexpectedly—and there's fresh linen on the bed. I'm afraid there's only one bedroom,' she went on, looking at them a little uncertainly, obviously not liking to ask directly about their sleeping arrangements. 'But the couch in the sitting-room doubles as a second bed, if you need it.'

'Yes, we'll need it,' Mae said firmly.

'Well, you'll find extra sheets in the cupboard in the bathroom. I'll leave you now to get settled in. Come and find me if there's anything else you need, or any questions you want to ask.'

She gave them a friendly smile, and then left them on their own. As soon as the door had closed behind her, Mae turned to Lyndon.

'Why did you say we'd stay here?' she demanded heatedly. 'You knew I didn't want to!'

'There's nowhere else on the island we can stay,' Lyndon pointed out calmly. 'And you are entitled to be here.'

'I don't know yet if I'm entitled to anything,' she retorted, flinging a black look at him. 'I won't know that until I've seen Malcolm Morgan.'

'And can you think of a better place to wait for him than here, at his own villa?' he said reasonably.

'You do realise that Mrs Matthews could lose her job because of us?' Mae demanded. 'When he finds out why we're here, I don't suppose he's going to be in the least pleased. And he isn't going to feel very well disposed towards Mrs Matthews when he discovers that she actually invited us to stay at his villa! Don't you care that that woman might end up unemployed because of us?'

Lyndon's gaze sharpened. 'Of course I care! And if it happens, I'll help her to find a similar job. I've got plenty of contacts. It shouldn't be too difficult.'

'Perhaps she doesn't want a similar job,' Mae said bitingly. 'Perhaps she wants *this* one. And I'm going to make sure she keeps it. I'm not going to be responsible for putting her out of work.'

She grabbed hold of her case and headed towards the door. Lyndon got there ahead of her, though, completely blocking it.

Mae shot a filthy look at him. 'Let me out of here!'

'You're not going anywhere,' he told her.

'Yes, I am! And you can't stop me.'

'Of course I can.' He reached behind him, turned the key in the lock, and then slid the key into his pocket.

She glared at him. 'Do you think that'll stop me getting out of here?'

'No. But it'll keep you here long enough to listen to what I've got to say.'

'I think I've listened to you for far too long. Ever since I met you, you've been telling me to do this, do that, go here, stay there. Well, I've had enough! I can run my own life and make my own decisions. I don't need you any more!'

Her yellow eyes shone with a fierce brilliance, and they didn't flinch before the brightness of his own gaze.

'You think that you don't need me?' Lyndon said in a terse voice. 'Then just answer me this. Where would you be *without* me?'

'I'd be back in my own flat, in London,' she yelled at him. 'I'd be going to work, getting on with my life. I'd be doing all the normal things that normal people do.'

'And at least once every day, you'd still be wondering who the hell your father was,' he said grimly.

That stopped her in her tracks, because he was right, of course. It was a question that she had been silently asking for the whole of her life.

'I'm the one who gave you the answer,' Lyndon reminded her, taking hold of her shoulders and shaking her a little roughly. 'I'm the one who brought you here, who made you stay when you wanted to run away, who actually got you right into Malcolm Morgan's villa. Now tell me again that you don't need me!'

Mae looked right into his eyes, and then shivered. This man knew far too much about her. She didn't like that. And she didn't like the way he was looking at her right now. It was as if he *wanted* her to need him. As if it satisfied some deep need of his own.

Slowly, his brilliant blue gaze still never leaving her face, he released her shoulders. Then he reached into his pocket and brought out the key.

'Do you want it?' he said softly. He held it in front of her. 'If you really want to leave, you can have it.'

But Mae was learning a few things about him by now. 'And what's your price for that key?' she said warily.

His mouth relaxed into an unexpectedly tired smile. 'So, you're finally learning that there's a price to be paid for everything? Perhaps that's good. It's a sign of maturity, when you start to face up to reality.'

'Tell me the price!' she repeated sharply.

'You already know it. I'll give you the key for nothing. All you've got to do is take it out of my hand. But once you put it in that lock, turn it and walk out that door, you're going to be paying for the rest of your life. To begin with, you'll have to live with the knowledge that you're a coward. That you came so far, and then couldn't face the final hurdle. But the biggest price of all will be the knowledge that you turned your back on the truth. That you had the chance to find out about your own past, but didn't have the guts!'

'I can see Malcolm Morgan at some other time,' Mae said in a low voice.

'Yes, you can,' agreed Lyndon. 'But you won't. If you walk away now, you'll just keep on walking. There'll always be some excuse for not seeing him, and in time you'll convince yourself that nothing I told you was the truth, anyway. That you've no reason to see him because there's no way he could ever be your father.'

Mae knew he was right. She hated to admit it, but she knew herself well enough to know that she couldn't ever go through all this again. Either she stayed on Lindos and saw Malcolm Morgan when he finally returned, or she would never see him.

She stared at the key in Lyndon's hand. It would be so easy to take it. To turn her back on all of this and try to forget any of it had ever happened.

Except that she wouldn't be able to forget it. Lyndon had made very sure of that.

'There are times when I really think I hate you,' she said in a suddenly exhausted voice.

'I know.' His own tone had also altered. 'And I don't like it when you feel that way about me, Mae. I don't like it at all.'

'Then why are you doing this to me?' she burst out. 'Why do you keep pushing me?'

'Because you can't quite make it on your own.'

'I know,' she retaliated bitterly. 'I need you. You've already told me that.'

'I wish you needed me in other ways, as well.'

His softly spoken words were so unexpected that she couldn't quite believe she had heard them. She raised her eyes to his again, and saw that the expression in them had changed quite dramatically.

Oh, no, she thought, half closing her eyes. I can't cope with this. Not on top of everything else.

'I don't think you really mean that,' she said flatly. She certainly *hoped* he didn't mean it. She just didn't need any more complications.

Lyndon shrugged. 'I do mean it. But you can put your mind at rest, I don't intend to do anything about it right now.'

That didn't put her mind at rest at all. What did he mean, he wasn't going to do anything about it right now? That she could relax for a couple of hours, but she was going to have to spend the next few days waiting for him to p unce on her?

Mae decided that arrangement didn't suit her at all. She felt a sudden need to get this sorted out right now.

'Let's get a few things straight,' she said in a blunt tone. 'All I'm interested in at the moment is meeting this man who you keep insisting is my father. I can't think about anything else. I'm not interested in anything else. Do you get the message?'

Lyndon looked at her thoughtfully. 'I'm not sure that you actually mean what you're saying,' he said at last.

She let out a great sigh of exasperation. 'I'm just not getting through to you, am I? Look, if you won't believe anything else, then believe this. Ninety-nine per cent of all the women you meet might find you absolutely irresistible, but I don't. I'm the one exception. You don't get to me in any way.' She suddenly glared at him. 'Do you understand now what I'm trying to say?'

'Yes, I understand it,' he agreed calmly. 'But it doesn't quite match up with the signals you're sending out.'

Mae stared at him suspiciously. 'What signals?'

For the first time, he looked faintly amused. 'You really don't know?'

'I wouldn't be asking, if I did,' she snapped back at him. She was already regretting that she had let this conversation go on for so long. She should have brought it to a halt a long time ago, just turning her back on him and walking away if he had tried to keep it going.

He was looking at her now in a way that distinctly disturbed her. His light blue eyes were quite unfathomable, and she didn't like that. She felt a lot safer when she could at least make some kind of guess as to what he was thinking.

'Every woman gives off signals,' he said at last. 'Some are very easy to read. The "come on" signal, the "hands off" signal—they're always immediately recognisable. The signals that you give off are a lot more subtle, though. Faint, even a little confusing. It's as if you want something, but won't allow yourself to admit it.'

'And you'd prefer it if I gave off a clear "come and get me" signal?' Mae said with deep sarcasm. 'Well, sorry to disappoint you!'

'Oh, I'm not disappointed,' Lyndon replied in an unruffled tone. 'I like subtlety in a woman. I particularly like it in you,' he went on in a suddenly huskier tone of voice.

Mae scowled at him. 'I don't want you to like *anything* in me!'

'Why not?'

His simple question unexpectedly threw her. 'Because—well, because——' She was annoyed to find that she couldn't come up with a single reasonable answer. Lyndon began to look amused, which irritated her even further. In a sudden burst of temper, she stamped her foot on the floor. Then she grabbed hold of her case, marched off into the small bedroom, and slammed the door shut behind her.

She felt rather better once Lyndon was out of sight. She was already regretting that last childish burst of temper, of course. She didn't want him to think that he was getting through to her in any way. It was partly her own fault, though, for not walking away from him earlier. Why on earth had she let herself get involved in that ridiculous conversation in the first place?

Restlessly, Mae walked over to the window. There was a small terrace outside, with a couple of tubs of flowers, and the view was stupendous. She could see right across the bay, with its bright blue water and its stunning backdrop of cliffs.

At any other time, she would have adored staying in a place like this. Not for one moment, though, could she forget whose house this was. Nor could she forget that Lyndon Hyde was standing outside that door, or that she was going to have to share this apartment with him for a couple of days.

Mae sighed, kicked off her sandals, and flopped tiredly down on to the bed.

Nothing seemed to be going right. Malcolm Morgan wasn't here, Lyndon was showing signs of becoming difficult to handle, and right at this moment she didn't feel up to coping with any of it. Too much had happened in too short a time. She hadn't had any chance to adjust to all the sudden changes in her life.

She gave another sigh, and closed her heavy eyes. Perhaps she would take a short nap. When she woke up, she might feel more refreshed and capable of dealing with all of this.

Instead, though, she fell into a deep sleep, and didn't wake up again until long after darkness had fallen.

CHAPTER FIVE

WHEN Mae opened her eyes, it was a couple of minutes before she could figure out where she was. Just enough moonlight was shining through the window for her to be able to see the dim outlines of the furniture, but nothing around her seemed familiar except for her suitcase, which she had dumped just inside the doorway.

Gradually, though, her sleepy head began to clear, and things began to fall into place. She was in Malcolm Morgan's villa. She was staying here with Lyndon Hyde. And, although it was the last place on earth she really wanted to be, she was going to have to spend the next couple of days here.

With a small groan, she dragged herself off the bed, switched on the light, and then looked at her reflection in the small mirror that hung on the wall.

A pale face with dark-rimmed eyes stared back at her, framed by a wild tangle of dark red curls.

'Not a pretty sight!' she muttered to herself. 'I need a long, hot shower. In fact, I think I need a complete overhaul!'

She supposed that this self-contained apartment had its own bathroom. She ran the risk of bumping straight into Lyndon if she went in search of it, though. And she really didn't feel like seeing him right now. In fact, she didn't think she would mind too much if she never saw him again!

In the end, though, Mae decided that she really did need that shower. Very cautiously, she eased open the door of the bedroom. With luck, Lyndon would be asleep. She could tiptoe past him, and he wouldn't even know she was there.

He wasn't in the sitting-room, though. A small lamp had been switched on, so she could see the room quite clearly. She could also see that the couch, where she had assumed he would be spending the night, was untouched.

Mae frowned. Where was he?

Then she remembered that last night, at the taverna, he had taken himself off for a long walk in the small hours of the morning. Perhaps it was something he did quite often. For all she knew, he might suffer from galloping insomnia. Anyway, she didn't really have to worry about where he was. He wasn't *here*, and that was all that really mattered.

There was a door on the far side of the sitting-room, but when she pushed it open she found it led into a small but well-equipped kitchen. There were signs that Lyndon had had something to eat, but the kitchen itself was empty. Mae gave a silent sigh of relief. He must have gone out.

There was just one door left to try. Confident that this one had to lead into the bathroom, Mae first went back to the bedroom and rummaged around in her suitcase until she had found soap, a towel, some talc, and a thin cotton nightie to put on after she had finished showering. With luck, once she was squeaky clean, and relaxed by the spray of hot water, she would be able to get a few more hours' sleep.

Feeling more cheerful than she had in a long while, she returned to the bathroom and pushed open the door.

The first thing she heard was the sound of running water. Mae frowned. Had Lyndon used the bathroom, and forgotten to turn off the tap?

Then she realised that he was *still* using it. It was the shower she could hear running, not a tap. And, since the shower curtain was extremely thin, it was all too easy to make out the shape of the tall male figure standing behind it!

Mae gulped audibly. At the same time, Lyndon drew back the shower curtain and stared at her with some interest.

She very hastily closed her eyes. 'Put on a bathrobe or—or something,' she spluttered.

'You can open your eyes again now,' Lyndon told her a few seconds later, his voice edged with bright amusement. 'I'm perfectly decent.'

Mae warily looked at him, and found that he hadn't exactly told her the truth. He was only halfway decent. He had a fairly small towel wrapped around his waist, which left an awful lot of his wet, naked body still on view.

And a fairly impressive view it was, she had to admit. Not that she was enjoying looking at him. Of course she wasn't! she told herself very firmly.

'I'll—er—come back when you've finished using the bathroom,' she muttered.

'There's no need for that,' Lyndon said casually. 'I don't mind sharing the shower.'

'Well, I do!' she shot back at once.

He raised one dark eyebrow. 'I didn't think you were the shy type.'

'I'm not. But that doesn't mean I want to share a shower with you.'

The corners of his mouth suddenly curved into a smile that was totally wicked. 'It could be a lot of fun.'

And it could also be highly dangerous! Mae decided at once. There might be a teasing note in his voice, but there was also a gleam in his light blue eyes that warned her that this could easily get out of hand.

With some determination, she began to move towards the door.

'Turning down my offer?' Lyndon challenged softly.

'In certain situations, I happen to like some privacy,' she retorted.

'So do I.'

She looked at him sceptically. 'That's pretty hard to believe. You've probably shared more showers with women than I've had hot dinners!'

Lyndon openly grinned. 'Not quite that many. Although I do remember one or two occasions that were rather spectacularly enjoyable. I wasn't lying when I said that I liked privacy, though.'

Mae snorted in disbelief. 'You'll be telling me next that you live like a monk!'

'Not quite,' he said drily. 'Although I do live on my own.'

'Well, I'm sure that's only a very temporary situation. I suppose you're between blondes, at the moment!'

'Lately, I find that blondes leave me cold. But I am very turned on by redheads,' he said in a silky tone. 'And if you're interested, I always live on my own.'

'I'm not in the least interested,' Mae shot back.

'I also sleep on my own,' he went on, as if she hadn't even spoken.

That made her eyes fly wide open. 'You *sleep* on your own?' she repeated in pure astonishment. Then she got a little more control over her voice. 'Now, that I *don't* believe,' she said flatly.

His mouth relaxed into a lazy smile. 'I'm not saying that I don't occasionally share my bed with anyone. Only that I like to sleep on my own afterwards.'

'Why?' asked Mae. She knew that she shouldn't be showing any curiosity in anything this man said or did, but somehow that one word just popped out before she could stop it.

Lyndon shrugged. 'I suppose it was because there was never any privacy during all the years I was growing up.'

'And where did you grow up?' That question, too, came out involuntarily. She thought he might not even answer it, because he didn't seem in the least keen on giving out personal information about himself. To her surprise, though, he seated himself on the edge of the bath and seemed quite prepared to go on with the conversation.

'I never seemed to stay in one place for very long,' he said. 'I got through several sets of foster-parents, and, when the authorities couldn't find anyone to look after me, they would shovel me back into a children's home for a few months until they could come up with someone who was willing to take me on for a while.'

Mae felt an unexpected pang of pity for him. 'That doesn't sound like much of a childhood,' she said in a much more sombre voice.

'It wasn't quite as bad as it sounds,' Lyndon replied. 'Kids are fairly resilient. And in those kind of circumstances you either learn to adapt and cope, or you go under.'

'And you're not the type to go under?' Mae said with a certain amount of grudging admiration.

'I'm still here, aren't I?'

'All the same, it couldn't have been much fun, not having a real home.'

'There were times when it wasn't any fun at all,' he agreed. 'But I made a lot of friends, and the people who looked after me were generally kind and under-standing. The only thing really lacking was any kind of privacy. I always had to share a room with other kids, and often I had to share a bed, as well. I don't have to do either of those things any more, and so I don't.'

Mae was silent for a while. He had made light of the whole thing, but she guessed there was a whole lot that he hadn't told her. She also guessed that an upbringing like that had to leave a lot of invisible scars. She, at least, had had one parent to raise her. Even so, it hadn't been at all easy, growing up without a father. She couldn't quite imagine what it would be like to have no one at all.

'You've gone very quiet,' Lyndon remarked.

'I was just thinking about one or two things,' she said slowly.

'Don't start feeling sorry for me,' he warned. 'I don't need that.'

She raised her eyes and looked at him. 'Do most people start feeling sorry for you?'

'Most people don't know anything about my back-ground. You're the first person I've talked to about this in years.'

That made Mae feel a little uneasy. She wasn't anyone special in his life, so it didn't make sense that he should confide in her like this. '*Why* have you told me all this?' she blurted out.

Lyndon got slowly to his feet and she remembered, rather too late, that he was very nearly naked. She should stop asking all these questions, and instead get out of here!

He was already answering her last question, though.

'Why have I told you?' he repeated thoughtfully. 'I suppose it's because we're alike, Mae. More than most other people, you can understand what I'm talking about.'

'We're not alike,' she insisted, for some reason deeply disturbed by his insistence that they were. 'I didn't spend my childhood with foster-parents or in children's homes. I've got a mother, remember?'

As soon as she had said those last words, she wanted to sink right through the floor. What on earth had made her say something like that! The last thing he wanted to be reminded of was the fact that he had no one at all!

'I'm sorry,' she muttered. 'Oh, hell, what a tactless thing to say!'

To her surprise, he didn't look angry. Instead, he actually gave her a faint smile.

'I don't mind tactlessness—at least, not when it comes from you,' he told her. 'And, yes, you've got a mother. But I've got the feeling that the two of you aren't very close.'

'She never let me get close!' Mae retorted. Then she gave a dark frown. She hadn't meant to tell him anything like that. Both of them seemed to be saying far too much tonight.

'Why didn't she let you get close?' he asked.

'I don't know,' she muttered. Then she scowled at him. 'You seem to like dabbling in amateur psychology. *You* give me an answer.'

He seemed about to say something. Then he obviously changed his mind. Instead, he moved a little closer and just stood there, looking at her.

'What are you staring at me like that for?' Mae demanded edgily.

'I've just decided that I've had more than enough of all these questions and answers for tonight,' he told her softly. 'What good does it do to keep rooting around in the past? We've got to live in the present. And, right now, I've got something rather different on my mind.'

Mae was just about to ask what it was when she caught the bright flare in the depths of his eyes, and she very hastily closed her mouth again. It might be a lot safer not to know! Anyway, any conversation with Lyndon always seemed to end up with her saying far more than she had ever meant to.

'I'm—er—going back to bed,' she said, her voice not coming out nearly as firmly as she had intended.

'You haven't taken your shower,' he reminded her.

'I'll shower in the morning.'

His blue gaze rested on her with new brilliance. 'Are you nervous because of me? Because of what you think I might do?'

'I'm not nervous at all!' Mae denied at once, at the same time hoping he couldn't see the gentle tremor that seemed to have set in around her knees.

'Would it help if I got dressed?' His light blue eyes were still very bright, but they were also lit with amusement now.

'As far as I'm concerned, you can sit around in that towel all night. It doesn't worry me in the least,' Mae lied, with as much bravado as she could muster. She certainly wasn't going to admit that she wasn't used to holding very personal conversations in the bathroom, in the middle of the night, with a man who was virtually naked!

She found herself noticing the way his skin shone in the soft glow of the light which illuminated the bathroom. It looked very supple, as if it would be warm and smooth to the touch——

Mae hastily caught hold of her wandering thoughts. She was tired, that was all, she excused herself. And confused after the long journey, and all the unsettling events of the last couple of days.

Lyndon moved towards her, and she nervously began to back away. She certainly didn't want him coming any nearer.

'I'm only getting my bathrobe,' he told her. 'It's hanging on the door behind you.'

She turned round, and saw the towelling robe hanging from the hook. Then she swung back and glared at him.

'Why didn't you put on your bathrobe straight away? Why have you been standing around in just that towel all this time?'

Lyndon glanced down, his expression perfectly innocent now. 'What's wrong with the towel?'

'It's—too small,' she got out through lips that were pursed thinly with disapproval.

He gave her a smile that was laced with pure wickedness. 'It seems perfectly adequate to me.'

'It hardly covers everything it's meant to cover,' Mae retorted. 'And don't smile at me like that! You can't charm *me* with a smile.'

His expression began to alter. 'Then what can I charm you with, Mae?' he asked softly.

'Nothing at all. I don't want to be charmed!'

His light blue gaze fixed on her face. 'Are you sure? It seems to me that there's an awful lot missing in your life.'

She was about to tell him that he didn't know anything at all about her life, but then remembered that he actually knew far too much. He had done all that research into her background; he knew a great deal more than she would ever have willingly told him.

'Let me guess what you think is missing from my life,' she said bitingly. 'Sex. That's it, isn't it? And I suppose you're offering to supply it!'

He continued to look at her consideringly. 'I'd certainly be quite willing, if that was what you wanted from me,' he said at last. 'I've already told you that I want you. Sex is very easy to supply, though. All you need is a little physical skill, and to be able to relax and enjoy it. I think you want something more than that, Mae. And I'm beginning to wonder if I can give it to you.'

'Well, you can just stop wondering,' she told him shortly. 'I don't want you to give me anything at all. In fact, I wish you weren't even here!'

She knew that she was being very rude now, but she didn't care. This bathroom was too small, too claustrophobic. Lyndon seemed to fill it with his presence—and it was a presence that could all too easily become overpowering. This man could effortlessly radiate strong waves of charm and sexuality—

and he certainly knew how to use that ability to his advantage. It was switched on now at full force. Mae could feel it radiating out from him. More annoying—and more disturbing—she could feel her own instinctive response to it. She hadn't expected that. She had thought she could stay immune to Lyndon Hyde, no matter what the circumstances.

He was studying her through slightly narrowed eyes now, as if gauging her response. Mae decided she had had enough of this. She clutched her towel, soap and nightie more tightly in front of her, as if they could somehow keep him at bay. Then she turned towards the door.

'Stay for a couple more minutes,' Lyndon said in a much quieter tone.

'What on earth for?' she snapped back sharply.

'We could talk for a while longer.'

Mae gave a small snort. 'I don't think that you want to talk!'

'No, you're right,' he agreed easily. 'I'd much rather do this.'

The kiss that followed was executed so smoothly and skilfully that Mae never had a chance to avoid it. And, once it had begun, she didn't see much point in struggling. He was far bigger and stronger than she was. This kiss would go on until he decided that it would end. Anyway, in her albeit limited experience, she had discovered that struggling only seemed to excite some men still further. It was much better to remain completely unresponsive. It usually got results, as well. Men soon gave up if a woman made it clear she was completely uninterested in them. Something to do with their male pride, she supposed.

And it wasn't difficult to remain unresponsive, either. Mae had always thought that kissing was a highly overrated activity. Some men were better at it than others, of course, but on the whole she had always found it very unexciting.

Lyndon didn't give up easily, but she had never expected that he would. And she had to admit that, on a scale of one to ten, he rated pretty high.

In the end, he released her mouth, and then just stood looking at her with a very thoughtful expression on his face.

Mae didn't like that. She would much rather that he had snarled something at her and then strode off.

'Get the message?' she said through gritted teeth. 'I'm not interested!'

'You're not interested because you're not enjoying it,' he replied calmly. 'And you're not enjoying it because you're far too tense.'

'What would you like me to do?' she retorted sarcastically. 'Try some yoga or meditation for half an hour beforehand, to relax me and get me in the right mood?'

'I don't think you need to go that far. There are other ways of relaxing.'

His voice positively purred over those last few words, and Mae actually found herself briefly wondering what ways he had in mind. Then, horrified that she should even think such a thing, she backed away and glared at him.

'Look, I don't want to kiss you, I don't want to kiss anyone. I don't like it and I'm no good at it.'

His dark eyebrows shot up. 'For heaven's sake,' he said with a first touch of impatience, 'it isn't something that you have to be *good* at. It's just something to be enjoyed.'

'Well, I don't enjoy it,' Mae said stubbornly. 'We could stand here kissing all night, and you still wouldn't get me to change my mind about that.'

'It's a very tempting proposition,' he murmured. 'But I don't think I could spend all night just kissing you. I'd want to move on to other things, and you're definitely not ready for that. Not yet.'

'You're right about that,' Mae retorted. 'And, as far as you're concerned, I'm *never* going to be ready.'

'Are you sure of that?' Lyndon asked silkily.

'Absolutely!'

Despite the note of complete conviction in her voice, he didn't look in the least convinced. That really annoyed her. Did the man think he was totally irresistible? Well, he certainly wasn't! He didn't get to her in any way at all.

Mae decided that she had had enough of this conversation. She had also had enough of Lyndon Alexander Hyde. She threw one last black look in his direction, then wheeled round and left the bathroom without saying another word to him.

Back in the safety of the bedroom, she threw her soap and towel on to a chair, wriggled out of her crumpled clothes, and crawled into bed without bothering to put on her nightdress. She still badly wanted a shower, but there was no way she was going to go back into that bathroom tonight. Instead, she resolutely closed her eyes, determined to go to sleep for a couple of hours and forget about Lyndon Hyde.

It wasn't as easy as she had expected, though. For some reason, she kept thinking about that kiss he had given her, and that irritated her immensely. It hadn't been *that* special. Very expert, of course, with no fumbling around, but Lyndon had never struck her as a man who would fumble at anything.

Mae thumped the pillow and tried to get more comfortable. The more determined she was to sleep, though, the more wide awake she became. In the end, she simply gave up. She switched on the bedside lamp, dug a paperback out of her case, and read until the sky began to glow with the pale light of the rising sun.

Perversely, now that it was time to get up, she began to feel sleepy. She didn't want to stay in bed all morning, though. She didn't feel particularly safe here, not with Lyndon only in the next room.

She got out of bed and pulled on her nightdress. Then she grabbed her towel and soap again, and headed towards the door.

She opened it silently, and then peered cautiously round it. To her relief, she saw that Lyndon was asleep. He was sprawled out on the couch, although it was obviously too small for him, and his feet trailed over the end. Good! Mae thought nastily. She hoped he had had a really uncomfortable night!

Since she had to pass him in order to get to the bathroom, she began to tiptoe past him. She stopped when she drew level with him, though, and stared down at him for a few moments.

His dark hair was tousled and he looked altogether far less intimidating than he did when he was awake. He was wearing just the bathrobe, which wasn't fastened very securely, so quite a lot of his body was on show. Mae had already seen virtually all of it, of course, in the bathroom last night. That didn't stop her having a good second look, though.

'Do you like what you see?' murmured Lyndon, without opening his eyes.

Mae jumped back several inches. Then she glared at him. 'You were only pretending to be asleep!' she said in an outraged tone.

One blue eye flickered open. 'I wanted you to be able to have a good look at me without feeling embarrassed,' he said with a wicked grin.

'I wasn't looking at you!' Mae denied instantly.

His eyebrows drifted upwards in clear scepticism.

'You don't think I'm *interested* in you, do you?' Mae went on heatedly. 'Not even you could be that conceited!'

His other eye had opened by now, and both of them were fixed on her red, flustered face.

'How could I possibly think you're interested in me?' Lyndon said cheerfully. 'After all, you keep telling me at some length that you're not.'

'And I mean it.'

'Of course you do.' His eyes flickered with amusement. 'I'm sure that you're not a girl who deliberately lies about anything.'

The implication behind his words was quite plain. She wasn't lying—she just hadn't realised yet that she wasn't quite as uninterested in him as she kept insisting.

Mae gave a snort of disgust. 'It's absolutely impossible to get through to a man like you. You're so used to women swooning at your feet that you can't accept someone might be immune to all that sexy charm.'

Then she blinked. She hadn't meant to say that! Sexy charm? What on earth had made her use a phrase like that? It definitely hadn't been a good choice of words.

'I'm going to take a shower,' she informed him icily. Then her yellow eyes became fierce again. 'And before you ask, no, I *don't* want you to join me.'

'I wasn't even going to suggest it,' Lyndon said, his gaze very bright now. 'A girl who doesn't like kissing certainly isn't going to enjoy sharing a shower. We've got to work on the more basic stuff before we get round to something like that.'

'*We* haven't got to work on anything,' Mae said hotly. 'I want to leave things exactly as they are. Haven't you got that message yet?'

Lyndon shrugged lightly. 'Just because you keep telling me something, it doesn't mean that I have to believe it.'

'Oh, you're impossible!' Mae snapped irritably, and she stalked off to the bathroom.

The shower was hot and refreshing, but she didn't enjoy it. She was in Malcolm Morgan's house, which in itself was enough to make her thoroughly uneasy, and on top of that she was sharing this apartment with Lyndon, which definitely set all of her nerves jumping at top speed. If she got through the next couple of days without having a complete nervous breakdown, she was going to be very lucky!

She got out of the shower and dried herself, then realised that she hadn't brought any clothes with her. She would have to put her nightdress back on. That made her frown darkly. She was sure it wasn't a good idea to be around Lyndon, wearing just a nightie.

She could hardly stay in the bathroom for the rest of the day, though. With a deep sigh, Mae wriggled into the nightie. She would walk straight past him, she decided firmly. And if he spoke to her, she would simply ignore him.

When she went back into the sitting-room, though, she found that Lyndon wasn't there. She gave a huge sigh of relief, shot quickly into the bedroom, and closed the door.

Ten minutes later, she was dressed in jeans and a T-shirt, and with her hair brushed into a fairly tidy tumble of curls. She was also starving hungry. She couldn't remember when she had last eaten a decent meal.

She quickly made her way to the kitchen. There was still no sign of Lyndon anywhere in the apartment. He must have dressed and gone out while she was in the shower. Mae began to relax just a little. At least she would be able to cook herself a meal and eat it without those light blue eyes fixed on her, ruining her appetite.

Half an hour later, she pushed her empty plate to one side and gave a small sigh of satisfaction. She was feeling much better now—almost capable of coping with life!

While she washed up the dirty plates and cutlery, she wondered what to do for the rest of the day. If she just sat around, she would only start to feel nervous all over again. The meeting with Malcolm Morgan still loomed in front of her, and every time she thought about it she began to shake gently inside.

She would go out for a couple of hours, she eventually decided. It was a gorgeous day. She would explore some of the island.

She left the apartment, and made her way through the main part of the villa. A door leading to one of the terraces stood wide open, so she went through and then stood in the sunshine for a couple of minutes, looking out over the curve of the bay. Malcolm Morgan had certainly picked a fantastic site for his villa. It must be marvellous to wake up to a view like this every morning.

The sound of someone calling her name brought her back to earth. She glanced down, and saw that Lyndon was making his way up the steep stone steps that led from the tiny beach far below all the way up to the villa.

'Oh, damn!' she muttered under her breath. Why did he have to turn up and ruin what had seemed like a perfectly nice morning?

When he reached the terrace, she saw that he must have been for a swim. His hair was still wet, and his skin glittered damply in the sunlight. He was wearing just a faded pair of jeans, which still left quite a lot of his body on show, but at least it was an improvement on the small towel that had barely covered him last night.

'Come on down to the bay,' he invited.

'No, thank you,' she said stiffly.

'Why not?' His eyes gleamed. 'You'll be quite safe,' he told her. 'You can see the beach from the villa. If I start to do anything you don't like, you can signal to Mrs Matthews and she'll come down to rescue you.'

'I don't need to be rescued from anyone,' Mae told him sharply. 'And particularly not from you!'

'Then why won't you come down to the bay? It's the most beautiful spot on the island,' he said persuasively.

Mae gave a small sigh. She supposed she might as well go. She certainly didn't want to stay inside the villa. Nor did she really want to go trudging round the dusty roads of Lindos on her own.

'Oh, all right,' she said, although without much enthusiasm.

'Do you want to swim?' asked Lyndon. 'If you do, bring a costume.'

'I haven't got one.'

'Nor have I,' he said with a grin. 'I hope Mrs Matthews wasn't too shocked, if she was looking out of the window!'

Mae looked at him warily. 'Are you planning on going swimming again?'

'Not this morning.' Then he grinned again as he saw the obvious look of relief on her face. 'Was the thought of seeing my naked body twice in the last few hours too much for you?'

'There's nothing very exciting about a naked male body,' Mae said with as much coolness as she could muster.

He looked at her quizzically. 'You have led a sheltered life, haven't you? But to get back to the question of a swimming costume. You can wear pants and a bra—they're as good as a bikini. And if you're feeling particularly modest, just put on an old T-shirt.'

'I don't want to swim,' she told him. Which wasn't quite the truth, but she certainly wasn't going to prance around in front of him in just a lace bra and a very skimpy pair of pants!

'It's up to you,' he said with a small shrug. 'But come on down to the bay, anyway.'

The series of stone steps which led down to the beach had been cut right into the cliff. They were fairly steep, and the sheer drop on one side made Mae feel increasingly dizzy.

When they were about a third of the way down, she stopped for a few moments. Lyndon turned back to her, took a look at her slightly pale face, and then held out his hand.

'Need something to hold on to?' he offered.

Mae would dearly have liked to have said no. Her head was really starting to swim, though, and so she reluctantly reached out and took hold of his fingers.

She immediately felt much better; much safer. Which was ridiculous, really, she thought to herself. No woman should feel safe around Lyndon Hyde!

They eventually reached the bottom, and she had to admit the dizzying climb down had been worth it. A small semi-circle of golden sand nestled into the curve of the bay, the cliffs loomed behind them, wild and beautiful, and the blue, blue sea stretched out towards the horizon.

Then it occurred to Mae that she would enjoy the view even more if she weren't clinging on to Lyndon's hand. When she tried to let go, though, he curled his fingers round hers and kept hold of her.

'Please don't do that,' she said uneasily.

'Why not?'

'Because I don't want you to!'

'Are you sure?' he asked calmly.

'Yes!' she said in a very definite tone.

To her relief, he released her. Then he settled himself on a nearby flat rock, sitting in an easy, cross-legged position and gazing out to sea.

Mae sat down a safe distance away from him. Lyndon didn't say another word, and after a while she began to wonder if she had offended him. Not that she was worried if she *had*, of course, she assured herself staunchly. That was really the very least of her problems, at the moment.

All the same, she shot a quick sideways glance at him as the silence between them stretched still further. He didn't look particularly angry or offended, but when he had that calm expression on his face, it was always impossible to guess what he was really thinking or feeling.

After a while, the silence began to get on Mae's nerves.

'Are you deliberately ignoring me?' she said edgily, at last.

His light blue eyes registered genuine surprise. 'Of course not. Do you think I'd do something like that?'

'Well, you've certainly been very quiet ever since we got here.'

He uncurled his legs, got up, and came over to sit beside her. Mae immediately regretted saying anything. She should have let the silence just stretch on and on. At least she had been relatively safe while he was sitting some way away, and taking no notice of her.

Did that mean she didn't feel safe now? Mae thought about it and discovered, to her surprise, that she actually felt quite relaxed. Perhaps she was getting used to having him around, she thought with a wry grimace. They had certainly spent a lot of time together over the last few days.

'I wasn't ignoring you,' Lyndon told her a few moments later. 'I was simply thinking over a couple of things.'

'What kind of things?'

'To begin with, whether I'd done the right thing, bringing you here.'

At that, Mae's eyes shot wide open. 'But you were the one who *made* me come,' she reminded him.

'I know. But I'm not sure that I had the right to force you into it, the way that I did.'

'It's a bit late now to come to that sort of conclusion!'

'But not too late to turn back.'

She stared at him. 'You're telling me that you think I should leave?'

'I'm telling you that you've got to realise that you do have a choice. To stay or to go.'

Mae shook her head. 'I don't believe I'm hearing this!'

He shrugged. 'It's simply that I don't want to get to the point where I'm taking over your life completely. I don't think that would be good for either of us.'

Now it was Mae's turn to stare out to sea for a while and do some serious thinking. Finally, she turned back to him. 'You might have pushed me into this, but a part of me must have *wanted* to be pushed, or I'd simply have told you to go away and not come back. I'm not a doormat, I don't let other people arrange my life for me. I'm here because, deep down, I do want to see Malcolm Morgan. I might be scared to death of finally meeting him face to face, I sure as hell don't know what I'm going to say to him, but I know that I can't leave Lindos until I've seen him.'

Her answer seemed to satisfy Lyndon, because he gave a brief nod and looked a lot more relaxed.

'And you are certainly not taking over my life,' she told him firmly. 'Not in any way.'

'I've already realised that I don't seem to be making much headway in certain directions,' he said drily.

'But I do have plans to change that,' he added in a rather different tone of voice.

Mae was instantly wary again. 'What kind of plans?'

He smiled lazily. 'If I told you, I'd lose the element of surprise. And I think that, where you're concerned, I need a few advantages on my side.'

'*You* need the advantages?' The amazement was clear in her voice.

'Of course I do,' he said equably. 'I told you that I wanted you, and I certainly haven't changed my mind about that. But getting you isn't going to be easy, Mae. I don't mind that, though. I've got a lot of patience, and I can wait as long as it takes.'

'You can wait a whole lifetime and still not get anywhere!' she retorted, jumping to her feet.

He seemed totally unruffled by her angry response, which exasperated her still further. He was so damned sure of himself! she thought angrily. Well, he was about to find out, perhaps for the first time in his life, that all that sexy charm wasn't quite enough. He had just run into a woman who found it quite resistible!

She stalked away from him and began to climb up the steep steps leading back to the villa. To her relief, he made no attempt to follow her. And when she reached the top she could still see him sitting there, gazing calmly out to sea like a man who was so sure of what he wanted—and his own ability to get it—that he could move at his own pace and pounce only when the time was exactly right.

CHAPTER SIX

MAE spent the rest of the day skulking in a shady corner of the terrace outside their apartment. She was partly trying to avoid Lyndon and partly making sure she stayed out of the sun. Her skin was too fair to tan easily. If she sat in the sun for too long, she knew she would turn as red as a lobster.

A couple of times she peered over the edge of the terrace, and saw Lyndon still lazing around on the beach far below. He obviously didn't have any problems with the sun, she told herself with some annoyance. He would be able to sit out in it for hours without burning, just going a deeper shade of golden brown. Mae felt a sharp pang of envy. One of the disadvantages of having dark red hair was that a really good suntan was just impossible.

Lyndon finally returned to the villa late in the afternoon. Mae stayed out on the terrace, hoping that he would go straight out again. She really didn't feel like facing him right now.

A few minutes later, though, he came out on to the terrace to find her. He was still wearing just a faded pair of jeans, and he looked completely relaxed.

And why shouldn't he? Mae muttered to herself silently. *He* wasn't here to face a man who might or might not be his father. He was only after an interesting angle to his feature on Malcolm Morgan. If he didn't get it, it wouldn't be the end of the world. He would just move on to another story, forgetting about Malcolm Morgan, about Lindos—and about her.

She looked up at him with sudden hostility. 'I'm sitting out here because I want to be on my own for a while!' she told him sharply.

Lyndon's eyes flickered briefly. Then he gave a brief shrug. 'That's OK by me. Everyone needs some time on their own, now and then.'

He turned round and went back into the villa, and Mae immediately felt an unexpected surge of disappointment. She hadn't thought he would go just like that, without even an argument. Then she gave herself an impatient shake. Wasn't that what she had wanted? she asked herself irritably. For him to go away, and leave her alone?

She wasn't very sure any more, and that rather unnerved her. She had the feeling that it was much better to know *exactly* what you wanted when you were around Lyndon Hyde. Otherwise you might find yourself being talked into doing what *he* wanted— and that could lead to all kinds of problems!

She stayed out on the terrace until the sun began to sink in the sky. Then she went into the kitchen, and cooked herself a meal. Lyndon had already eaten. She was surprised to find that he seemed very much at home in the kitchen. She supposed that the kind of childhood he had had, though, had made him fairly self-sufficient. And, of course, he lived alone. If he didn't want to eat out every night—and not many people wanted to do that—then he either had to learn to look after himself, or go very hungry!

After she had eaten, Mae decided to take herself off to bed. She was dog-tired after the sleepless nights she had had lately, and fell asleep only a couple of minutes after collapsing on to the bed.

In the morning, she woke up feeling more refreshed, but with her nerves still on edge. She had felt like that ever since Lyndon had told her the name of her father. She just wanted to get that first meeting with him over with. Why couldn't Malcolm Morgan have been here when they arrived? she asked herself crossly. Then it would have been over by now. One way or another, she would know the truth.

She showered and dressed, made herself a quick breakfast, and carried it on a tray out on to the terrace.

Lyndon was already sitting there, in the early morning sunshine. Mae nearly went straight back into the villa again when she saw him, but at the last moment she changed her mind. She could hardly keep running away from him. From now on, though, she was definitely going to try and keep some distance between them. Just lately, he kept getting far too close for comfort, and she didn't like it!

She sat at the small table at the far end of the terrace, and began to eat, although her appetite seemed to be fading fast. Lyndon watched her for a couple of minutes, his light blue eyes looking very relaxed. Then he gave a lazy smile.

'You've obviously decided that you can't avoid me completely. Just how close are you going to allow me to get?'

It always irritated—and unnerved—her when he so accurately guessed the thoughts inside her head.

'I don't know what you're talking about,' she said stiffly.

'Of course, you could always ask me to move out of the villa altogether,' he went on, as if she hadn't even spoken. 'But my guess is that you don't want to do that. You might not be too thrilled at having me around, but it's better than being at Malcolm Morgan's villa all on your own.'

Mae tried to swallow her coffee, but had trouble getting down more than a couple of small mouthfuls. He couldn't possibly know *everything* she was thinking, she told herself edgily. He was just making a couple of lucky guesses, that was all.

To her relief, he didn't say anything more. He still kept looking at her, though. Mae was about to tell him to find something else to stare at, but, at the last moment, changed her mind. She didn't want him to think that she was unsettled by a single thing that he said or did.

Somehow, she managed to finish her breakfast. As soon as she had pushed away her empty plate, though, Lyndon got to his feet and sauntered over. Mae felt her pulses give a hard, heavy thump, but ignored them. She didn't care how close he came, she told herself staunchly. She could cope with it. It wasn't going to become a problem.

Lyndon sat himself down in the chair opposite her. 'What do you want to do today?' he asked her. 'We can go out for a couple of hours, or we can stay here and wait for Malcolm Morgan to return.'

Mae's heart gave a sudden lurch. 'You think he'll be back today?' she asked edgily.

'I shouldn't think so. I doubt if we'll see him for another couple of days. I didn't know if you wanted to stick close to the villa, though, on the off chance that he'll come back early.'

But Mae didn't at all like being in this villa. She didn't feel that she had any real right to be here, and every minute she spent under Malcolm Morgan's roof seemed to set her nerves a little further on edge.

'I want to go out,' she said at once. Then she gave a small grimace. 'But I don't suppose there's anywhere much to go on this island.'

'There's one place that you might find interesting,' Lyndon said casually.

'Where?'

'Get yourself ready, and I'll take you there.'

She wasn't sure that she wanted to go anywhere with Lyndon, though.

'I might want to go out on my own,' she argued.

'You might,' he agreed. 'But it isn't much fun, tramping around a strange place by yourself.'

He had a point there. 'Oh, all right, I'll come with you,' she said reluctantly.

Ten minutes later, they left the villa. Lyndon seemed to know exactly where he was going, but, despite several rather exasperated questions from Mae, he wouldn't tell her where he was taking her. She very nearly changed her mind about going with him, and decided instead to return to the villa. She didn't go, though. If she had a choice between staying with Lyndon and returning to Malcolm Morgan's villa, then Lyndon won by a very narrow margin.

They followed a dusty track for some time, with Mae falling slightly behind as Lyndon set an unexpectedly fast pace. She almost had to run to catch up with him, and shot a dark look at him as she finally fell in alongside him.

'I didn't know this was going to be a route march!'

'Sorry,' he said cheerfully. 'I forgot that you aren't very fit.'

That immediately riled her still further. 'I'm perfectly fit,' she informed him. 'I just don't see any point in charging about at top speed in all this heat.' Then she looked at the canvas holdall slung over his shoulder. 'What have you got in that bag?' she asked curiously.

'Just a few things that we might need,' he replied, but wouldn't volunteer any more information.

Mae gave a silent sigh. She had the feeling that coming with him this morning had been a definite mistake. It was too late to turn back now, though. She wasn't even sure that she could find her way back to the villa without Lyndon's help.

They walked on for several more minutes, not saying anything more, but the silence stretching between them not feeling at all uncomfortable. The track began to wind round a fairly high hill, with the bushes and stunted trees that covered the hillside parting occasionally to give distant glimpses of the sea.

Then Lyndon stopped. 'This must be it,' he said.

Mae looked around, but couldn't see anything at all except for a stone marker at the side of the track.

'What exactly am I meant to be looking at?' she demanded. 'There's nothing here!'

Lyndon wasn't listening to her, though. Instead, he was pushing his way past a couple of bushes at the side of the track.

With a small shrug of exasperation, Mae followed him. The hillside rose above them steeply at this point. As far as she could see, they were making their way towards a blank wall of rock!

'This isn't exactly my idea of a good day out,' she remarked acidly. Then she realised that she was talking to herself. Lyndon had disappeared.

Mae swallowed hard. Where had he gone? How could he have vanished so quickly?

Then he reappeared in front of her, seeming to step out from the rock itself.

'This is it,' he announced. 'Want to have a look inside?'

She walked forward a few more steps, and then saw the dark, narrow hole in the hillside.

'It's a cave,' she said in a flat tone.

'Mrs Matthews told me about it, and gave me directions on how to find it,' said Lyndon.

Mae looked at him a little disbelievingly. 'You've brought me all this way to see a cave?'

'Step inside,' he invited. 'It's a lot more interesting than it looks from the outside.'

'Well, that wouldn't be difficult,' Mae commented. 'From here, it looks just like a hole in the hill!'

Lyndon was already disappearing back through the entrance, though. Mae gave a small sigh; then she followed him inside.

The natural light penetrated for only a few yards. Then black shadows began to gather, making it impossible to see any further.

Mae stopped just inside the entrance. 'Yes—very interesting,' she said, without the least hint of enthusiasm in her voice. 'Can we go back now?'

'We haven't seen anything yet,' Lyndon pointed out.

'There doesn't seem to be very much *to* see!' she retorted.

'That's because we haven't gone far enough.'

'It's far enough for me.'

Lyndon walked back to her. 'Do places like this make you feel claustrophobic?' he asked.

'No, they don't. But that doesn't mean I want to spend any time in them!'

He caught hold of her wrist. 'Stop complaining, and come and take a closer look.'

'At what?' she demanded, digging in her feet as he began to pull her forward. 'It's just a cave. A cold cave,' she added, feeling the chill air brushing against her skin. Then something icy hit her bare arm, and she gave a small shriek. 'And a *wet* cave!'

'Don't make such a fuss about a few drips of water,' he said with a touch of impatience. He began to walk forward again, towing her along behind him, even though she was still protesting. The floor of the cave began to slope steeply downwards, and Mae had to concentrate on keeping her balance because the ground was quite uneven.

'I can't see,' she grumbled, as they went further into the darkness.

Lyndon dug into the bag hooked over his shoulder, and brought out a powerful torch. 'That's why I brought this,' he told her.

The beam shone out ahead of them, clearly illuminating the way. It also showed her that the cave was widening out into a large underground chamber. Then Mae caught her breath as the torchlight danced over something else; something that loomed above them, dark and frightening.

'What is it?' she whispered, instinctively clutching hold of Lyndon's arm.

He shone the torchlight upwards, and she saw it was a great cluster of stalactites, hanging down like a huge frozen chandelier.

Lyndon urged her forward a few more yards, and Mae saw that the roof of the cavern was covered with the stalactites, the long icicles forming fantastic patterns. And from the floor of the cave equally awe-inspiring stalagmites grew up to meet them, sometimes joining up to form thin, elegant pillars.

It was a dark, dripping, spooky and yet beautiful place. They picked their way slowly through the cavern, Mae hardly aware that she was still clinging tightly on to Lyndon's arm. When they reached the far side, they could see another series of smaller caves stretching further into the hillside, but Lyndon didn't attempt to go any further.

'It would be very easy to get lost in here,' he said quietly. 'I think we'd better stay in the main cavern.'

Mae was quite happy to go along with that. She couldn't think of anything more frightening than being lost in a place like this.

Lyndon let the torchlight flicker over the fantastic frozen shapes that surrounded them. 'Impressive, isn't it?' he said at last.

'It certainly is,' she breathed, looking up at a delicate cluster of stalactites right above them. Then she jumped with shock as several icy cold drips cascaded down on to her face.

Lyndon smiled. Then he leant forward and licked the water off her cheek.

Mae jumped almost as much as she had when the water had first hit her. 'Don't do that!' she spluttered.

He looked at her lazily. 'Why not?'

'Because I don't like it!'

'Liar,' he said calmly. 'You didn't mind it at all.'

The most unnerving thing of all was that he was right. Mae was never going to admit that to him, though.

Rather belatedly, she realised that she was still clutching on to his arm. Very hurriedly, she let go of him. 'Well, we've seen the cave,' she said, making a huge effort to keep her voice steady. 'We can go now.'

'But I like it here,' Lyndon said in an unruffled tone. 'I'd like to stay for a while longer.'

'Then you can stay here on your own!'

'I've got the torch,' he pointed out. 'You won't get very far on your own in the dark.'

Mae's mouth set into an obstinate line. He was *not* going to keep her down here against her will. This place was too isolated. She guessed that hardly anyone ever came here. Anything could happen, and no one would ever know about it.

'Keep the torch,' she told him defiantly. 'I don't need it. I can get out of here without it.'

She began to walk away from him, but after only a few yards she had moved out of the pale circle of the torchlight and the darkness began to close in around her. Mae gritted her teeth and refused to give in. She just had to keep going, and eventually she would get back to the cave entrance.

She tripped and stumbled a few times over the uneven floor of the cavern, and then let out a loud yelp as she cracked her knee on a low stalagmite that she hadn't seen in the darkness.

Lyndon's voice floated over to her. 'It would be a lot easier if you came back here—to me.'

Mae muttered something very rude under her breath; then she doggedly started moving forward again.

'You're going in the wrong direction,' Lyndon told her. 'If you want to get out of this cavern, you need to head to your right.'

She glanced back at him, and saw he was sitting placidly on a flat piece of rock. The pale torchlight made his hair seem darker, and his features more starkly defined. He wasn't making any effort to come after her, probably because he knew he didn't have to. She wasn't going to get out of here on her own. She would have to go back to him, and let him guide her out by the light of the torch.

Mae hated giving in to him, but she was beginning to realise that it was futile to struggle on in the darkness. All the same, she didn't give up straight away. She managed to grope her way another half a dozen yards forward, and it was only when she cannoned into a tall group of stalagmites and then stubbed her toe badly that she finally gave in.

She had yelled out loud when she stubbed her toe. Lyndon immediately stood up and began to make his way towards her. Mae stood still and waited for him, a sulky expression on her face. She felt like a small child who had behaved badly, and she didn't like it. After all, *she* wasn't the one who was in the wrong. He was the one who had brought her down here, and then wouldn't show her the way out again when she had wanted to leave.

'Red hair usually goes with a fierce temper,' Lyndon remarked, as he finally reached her. 'But in your case, it seems to denote stubbornness.'

'Just because I don't like being licked,' Mae muttered angrily.

Lyndon's eyebrows rose gently. 'I hardly touched you.'

'There was no need to touch me *at all*.'

Even by the pale light of the torch, she could see the change in his eyes.

'I don't think you should lecture me on what I need until you know the meaning of the word.'

'I know it,' she insisted.

'Do you?' An odd smile touched the corners of his mouth. 'Somehow, I don't think so.'

There was something about his tone of voice that made Mae respond heatedly. 'Of course I do. It's a simple enough word. Everyone knows the meaning of it!'

'Then touch my hand,' said Lyndon, holding it out to her, palm upwards.

Mae looked at him warily. 'What for?'

'Just touch it,' he instructed.

She gave a small sigh. What was he up to now? Whatever it was, perhaps it would be better to get it over with quickly. She laid her own palm against his own, and then stared at him defiantly. 'All right, what now?'

'What do you feel?' he asked.

'Nothing,' she said promptly. Which wasn't altogether true, but she definitely wasn't going to let him know that.

She decided that this physical contact between them had gone on for long enough, and began to remove her hand. Lyndon closed his fingers over hers, though, and then looked straight into her eyes.

'You haven't asked me what *I* feel,' he said softly.

'That's because I'm not interested in knowing,' she retorted.

He gave that strange smile again. 'I'm going to tell you, anyway. I can feel the warmth of your skin, and the blood pulsing through your veins. I can feel the beat of your heart, and hear the thoughts inside your head.' His voice had taken on a low, almost hypnotic quality, and Mae couldn't tear her gaze away from the bright light in his eyes. 'I can feel my own blood getting hotter, and the ache in my fingers because they want to touch more than just your hand. And I can feel the ache in the rest of my body because it wants to move closer and touch and caress. That's what it's like to *need*, Mae. And if you really don't know what it feels like, then I feel rather sorry for you.'

'I don't want you to feel sorry for me!' she said in a prickly tone. At the same time, she was fighting hard to subdue a funny feeling deep inside of her. It was a warm sensation, a new sensation. She wasn't sure if she liked it, and she certainly didn't trust it because it made her feel peculiarly vulnerable.

Lyndon looked at her intently, and Mae quickly lowered her gaze. You could see far too much by looking straight into someone's eyes. He put one finger under her chin, though, and firmly raised her face until she was looking at him again.

'Do you understand any of what's happening between us?' he asked her, his own gaze very direct.

'No,' she said at once. 'But that's because nothing *is* happening,' she added defiantly.

'Yes, it is,' Lyndon replied calmly. 'But you're too inexperienced to recognise it.'

'Well, that's certainly something that you don't suffer from, is it? Inexperience!'

'Does that bother you?'

'Nothing about you bothers me,' she yelled back at him in sudden frustration. 'Except being stuck in this dark, creepy cave with you!'

He gave a suddenly wolfish grin. 'I like bringing you to places where you can't run away from me. It makes it a lot easier for me to do this.'

The kiss that followed wasn't exactly unexpected, and yet it still came as quite a shock. Perhaps it was because Mae was a lot less indifferent to it than she had expected. Or perhaps it was because he didn't seem to want to stop at just a kiss this time.

The restless pressure of his mouth was accompanied by the expert touch of his fingers, moving over her from one warm pleasure-spot to another. Mae meant to protest—and quite vehemently!—but there just didn't seem to be any opportunity. And she was beginning to realise that she could quite easily reach the point where she didn't even want to. That was definitely very alarming!

His kisses deepened, and his hands began to move over her with an easy familiarity, as if she already belonged to him. She could feel his fingers brushing against the curve of her breast, and she gulped hard. She had to stop this, before she actually began to like it!

Lyndon obviously didn't want to stop, though. When she tried to pull away, he simply moved with her, so that there was no escape from the warmth and closeness of his body. And his kisses went on and on, until she felt as if she were almost drowning in the flood of sensation that they seemed to be provoking inside her.

When he finally raised his head and released her, she was breathing as unevenly as he was. More disturbing than that, though, she felt *different*. Not at all the same person who had walked into this cave only a short time ago.

Lyndon looked into her dazed yellow eyes, and then smiled. 'I think that you enjoyed it far more this time.'

'I did not,' Mae croaked with a last feeble attempt at defiance, but it was an outright lie, and they both knew it.

'You enjoyed it because you feel more relaxed with me now,' Lyndon went on. 'You're getting used to having me around.'

'Well, that's not difficult,' Mae retorted, finally beginning to recover a little. 'You're around twenty-four hours a day!'

'Not quite,' he said easily. 'So far, we haven't spent any nights together.'

'And we're not going to,' she muttered, but somehow there wasn't quite the conviction in her voice that she had intended. Annoyed—and unsettled—by that, she shuffled her feet edgily. 'Are we going to leave this cave now?'

'If you want to.'

'I certainly do,' she said, and was relieved to find that her voice had come out much more firmly this time.

Lyndon led the way, and Mae stumbled along behind him, tripping up a couple of times on the uneven ground. She felt oddly uncoordinated, as if her body wouldn't quite obey her.

After she had tripped for the second time, Lyndon stopped and turned back to her.

'Want to hold my hand?' he invited, stretching out his fingers towards her.

Mae had already begun to move her hand towards his when she suddenly realised what she was doing.

'No!' she said sharply, very hurriedly snatching her hand back again.

Lyndon seemed unworried by her response. He simply gave a relaxed shrug, and then began to move forward again.

It seemed like ages to Mae before they finally reached the cave entrance and moved out into the sunshine, although it could only have been a few minutes. She blinked a little dazedly in the brightness, and hoped that things would now return to normal. That cave had been dark and spooky, she told herself firmly. *That* was what had made her behave the way she had.

'I wonder why more people don't come here?' she said, glancing around rather uneasily as she realised just how deserted this place was. 'I'd have thought this would be a favourite spot for tourists. Caves like this are usually quite an attraction.'

'The cave's on private property,' Lyndon told her. 'All the land around here belongs to the villa. That means it's all owned by your father.'

Mae's already raw nerves jumped. 'Don't call him that!'

'Why not?' asked Lyndon reasonably. 'It's what he is.'

'No one's proved that yet.'

'As far as I'm concerned, *I've* proved it. Although getting him to admit it might be another thing,' he said drily. Then he gave her a gentle shake. 'Come on, I think you've had enough for one day. Let's get back to the villa.'

'*His* villa,' she muttered.

'Just keep remembering that you've got every right to be there.' When she still didn't move, he caught hold of her hand and gently began to pull her along. This time, Mae didn't even try to yank her hand away.

Instead, she walked along beside him docilely, not making any effort to say anything more. He was right, she had had enough for one day. She felt tired, very drained, and in need of a strong shoulder to lean on for a while. She didn't even care who that shoulder belonged to. Not even if it was Lyndon Hyde's.

They eventually arrived back at the villa, and went straight to their apartment. The hot midday sun was pouring through the window, and Lyndon pulled down the blind. Then he walked back to Mae.

'Still feeling relaxed?' he asked her in a soft voice.

Suddenly much wider awake, she stared at him warily. 'Why?'

'Because I feel like kissing you again,' he answered easily.

'Well, you can't,' she shot back at once.

'Want to give me a good reason why not?'

Mae spent several seconds rather frantically trying to think of one. Then she realised that she didn't have to give him a reason at all.

'I just don't want to,' she said stiffly.

'I think that you do.'

She licked her dry lips. How had he known that? And *why* had she suddenly started to feel so differently towards him?

'Kissing only leads to—other things,' she said in a stilted voice.

At that, Lyndon gave a wolfish grin. 'I certainly hope so.'

'This isn't a good time. And it certainly isn't a good place,' she argued, backing away from him a little.

With one easy stride, he closed the distance between them again. 'It seems an excellent time to me,' he murmured. 'And the place isn't important. You're the only thing that's important.'

'I don't understand why I'm important,' she muttered.

Lyndon gave a brief shrug. 'Nor do I. I can't explain it. Who can? I just know that I want you. Ever since I first saw you, I wanted you.'

Her yellow eyes fixed on him. 'Wanting isn't enough.'

'I know that. But it's all I'm prepared to admit to, for now. If you pushed me, you could probably make me say more, but I don't want to. Not yet. This is already moving almost too fast. Let's take it one step at a time, and start with the simple things.'

'Like sex?' Mae said bluntly.

Lyndon gave a dry smile. 'Do you think that sex is simple? It can be the most complicated thing in the world. Especially when your emotions are involved. It's only simple when two people come together for nothing more than a couple of hours of physical pleasure.'

She looked at him warily. 'And that isn't what you want?'

'Oh, yes, I want it,' he told her softly. 'But not just for a couple of hours. I want it to last, and I want it to be good, and I want it to be special.'

There was a light in his blue eyes that she had never seen before. Mae felt as if she was having more than a little trouble breathing, and she certainly couldn't quite believe that they were having this conversation. It was far too personal, and too—well, too *intimate*. She needed to distance herself from this man, and get back to normal.

Except that she wasn't quite sure what passed for normal any more. The day seemed to have turned topsy-turvy. Nothing was quite the same as it had been this morning.

When had it changed? she wondered. When he had kissed her in that cave? But it had been just an ordinary kiss—hadn't it?

'Trying to figure it all out, Mae?' Lyndon challenged her quietly. 'Perhaps it would be easier if you just relaxed, and accepted it.'

'You're always telling me to relax,' she muttered. 'And it's about the most difficult thing on earth to do, when you're around!'

'No, it isn't,' he replied. 'Come over here, and I'll show you how to relax.'

But Mae stubbornly stayed where she was. She just couldn't bring herself to make that first move towards him.

Lyndon smiled. 'All right, then I'll come to you.' Before she could tell him she didn't want him to do that, he had walked over to her and placed himself behind her.

Mae became very tense. What was he going to do now? She soon discovered that he had nothing very alarming in mind. He simply placed his fingers on the taut muscles at the nape of her neck, and gently began to massage the tension out of them.

She found that the sensations his fingers induced were very nice. In fact, *more* than nice. She gave a soft, involuntary sigh of pleasure, and then stiffened again a little as she realised he must have heard it. It really wasn't at all sensible to behave like this, she lectured herself, although without much conviction.

'Just let go,' Lyndon murmured in her ear. 'Forget about all your problems. This is the only thing that's important, at the moment.'

Mae tried to remind herself that Lyndon *was* one of her problems, but it was getting harder and harder. He stopped massaging her neck, and his hands instead slid around her waist. He was still standing behind her, and she could feel his breath, warm and steady, against her hair.

He pulled her gently back against him, and she tried to break away, but only half-heartedly. His hands locked round her, keeping her firmly against him. Mae suddenly abandoned the struggle. She was tired of all this conflict. It was so much easier just to let go.

His hands moved up to the softness of her breasts, and she was amazed at how nice it felt to be touched so gently and intimately. He caressed her through the soft cotton of her T-shirt, but then seemed to become impatient with the thin barrier beneath his fingers. His hands slid under the T-shirt, and Mae caught her breath as his palms rubbed lightly against her bare skin.

'Do you like this?' he asked huskily. '*I* certainly like it, Mae. I've wanted to touch you like this since the day I first set eyes on you.'

Mae was only half listening. How could this be happening? she asked herself dazedly. And with Lyndon? And why wasn't she trying to stop it?

Before she had time to answer even one of those questions, he lightly nibbled the tip of her ear. Then he burrowed under her hair until his mouth found the soft, vulnerable skin at the base of her throat.

Mae was just hazily wondering where this was all going to end when the door to the apartment was suddenly flung open.

She jumped violently, her relaxed muscles instantly tensing up again. Lyndon moved more slowly, sliding his hands from under her T-shirt, and then coming to stand beside her.

Both of them looked at the man who had just stridden into the apartment. He was powerfully built, with short dark red hair and eyes that looked more amber than yellow in the shaded room. He stood and stared at Mae for a couple of moments. Then open contempt showed on his strong-featured face.

'So, you're the two who tricked your way in here,' he said in a harsh voice. 'And I've only got to take one look at the girl and I can guess why you're here. It's a stunt that's been pulled before, and more than once. I didn't fall for it then, and I'm not going to fall for it now.'

Mae tried to swallow, but couldn't. Her throat was too dry. 'You're—you're Malcolm Morgan?' she said in a cracked voice.

'Yes, I am,' he agreed grimly. 'I'm also the man who's about to throw you out of here.'

CHAPTER SEVEN

LYNDON stepped forward. 'I don't think you know who you're talking to,' he said evenly.

Malcolm Morgan made a sound of disgust. 'I don't care who you are. I don't even want to know your names.' His yellow gaze swung round to fix on Lyndon. 'How long did it take you to find a girl with the right colourings? A few weeks? A few months? I suppose you thought it would be worth all the trouble, considering the possible rewards if you succeeded in passing her off as my daughter.'

Mae managed to find her voice. 'I want to get out of here,' she muttered to Lyndon fiercely. 'And I want to go *right now.*'

'Not yet,' said Lyndon tightly. He turned back to Malcolm Morgan. 'I think you ought to know who she is.'

'Her name isn't important. *She* isn't important,' he said harshly. 'Oh, it was clever,' he went on, 'finding a girl of her age who looked just right. In the past, con men like you have always tried to hit me with a paternity suit. They confront me with a red-haired baby, and a red-eyed mother who keeps crying very prettily all the time she's trying to convince me that the baby is the result of a couple of nights we've spent together. This is the first time I've been presented with a fully grown adult trying to pass herself off as my child. I might almost admire your initiative, if I didn't think you were beneath contempt!'

Mae flinched, as if his words had physically hurt her. Lyndon immediately laid his hand on her arm, as if silently telling her that he was still here; she wasn't on her own. Then he looked back at Malcolm Morgan, his blue eyes absolutely icy.

'You've no right to speak to her like that.'

Malcolm Morgan's own gaze glittered. 'I think that I've every right. You tricked your way into my house, you've eaten my food, and when I walked in you were obviously about to make love on my bed. I don't allow even my close friends to behave like that.'

'I very much doubt if you have any close friends,' Lyndon said in a biting tone.

Mae looked up at him. 'Stop it,' she said, in a low voice. 'I don't want this to go any further.' She turned to Malcolm Morgan and, with difficulty, stared straight at him. 'We're leaving,' she said in a very clear voice. 'I don't want to stay in this house—*your* house—for one minute longer.'

For just one moment, as he stared back into her yellow eyes that were so like his own, a flicker of doubt seemed to show momentarily on Malcolm Morgan's face. Then it disappeared, and the dark, totally hostile expression returned.

'Mrs Matthews will pack your things,' he said shortly. 'You can collect them later. Then I strongly suggest that you leave this island as soon as you possibly can. I've a great deal of influence around here. If you're still here after a day or two, I'll have you arrested and slung into gaol.'

Lyndon slid his hand under Mae's elbow, and began to guide her in the direction of the door. Mae was very glad of his support. Her legs were trembling quite badly by now.

As they drew level with Malcolm Morgan, Lyndon turned and fixed him with his steady blue gaze.

'You're the one who'll be the loser if you throw us out,' he said evenly.

'Just get out of here,' said Malcolm Morgan shortly. 'Get out right now!'

Lyndon didn't flinch under the fierce yellow gaze. Nor did he leave immediately. Instead, he stared right back at Malcolm Morgan. To Mae's astonishment, Malcolm Morgan was the first one to look away. Only then did Lyndon continue to walk out of the apartment.

Once they were outside the villa, Mae visibly began to shake.

'Don't let him get to you,' Lyndon advised.

'That's easy for you to say,' she retorted edgily. 'You haven't been treated like a piece of dirt by someone who's probably your father!' Then she realised that wasn't a very tactful thing to say to a man who was *never* going to know who his father was. 'Sorry,' she muttered.

'It's all right,' he replied in a more relaxed tone. 'I don't mind if you're a little tactless now and then. The only thing I would mind is if you ignored me completely.'

'That would be rather difficult to do!'

'I'm glad to hear it.' Then his voice changed, and became more brisk. 'And don't get too upset about what just happened. The first meeting between the two of you was bound to be rather traumatic. We've given him something to think about, though. Next time, I think he'll be more willing to listen and behave reasonably.'

At that, Mae's head snapped up. '*Next* time?' she repeated. 'But I don't want to see him ever again!'

'Not now, you don't,' agreed Lyndon. 'But when you've calmed down, you'll look at it differently.'

'I won't,' she insisted fiercely.

His light blue gaze rested on her levelly. 'Now that you've seen him, what do you think? Do you believe that Malcolm Morgan is your father?'

It was a question that she didn't want to answer. In the end, though, she forced herself to think about it. She supposed she was going to have to face it sooner or later, so it might as well be now.

'Yes, I do,' she said at last, very reluctantly. 'How else could I look so much like him?'

'There's one way to be absolutely certain,' he told her. 'You could ask your mother.'

'No,' Mae said sharply. Then, in a lower tone, she repeated, 'No. I won't do that.'

'Are you going to tell me why?'

'I suppose so,' she said, with some resignation. 'I've told you just about everything else, haven't I?'

'Not quite. You haven't told me how you feel about me.' When her yellow eyes shot wide open, he gave a small shrug. 'All right, I know this isn't the right time. Let's get back to your mother. Why can't you simply ask her if this man is your father?'

'Because I'm fairly sure she wouldn't tell me, even if he was. When I was younger, I used to ask endless questions about my father, but she would never answer any of them. In fact, it was even worse than that. She would totally ignore me when I asked those questions. She'd cut herself right off from me, she behaved as if I weren't even there. I hated that, it really used to scare me, so in the end I stopped asking any questions at all.'

'You were a child then,' Lyndon reminded her. 'Now, you're an adult. Surely that makes a difference?'

'I don't know,' Mae said, biting her lip. 'I suppose I've always been afraid to start asking questions again, in case it puts even more of a distance between us. We've never been really close. She wouldn't *let* me get close. And I've always been frightened of doing something, or saying something, that would drive us even further apart.'

'Perhaps this would be a good time to try and establish a better relationship—a more mature relationship—with her,' he suggested.

'Maybe,' she said uncertainly. 'I just don't want to do anything that will make things worse between us.'

'Is that why you haven't had any serious boyfriends?' asked Lyndon. 'You couldn't find anyone you thought she would approve of?'

'I suppose so,' Mae admitted reluctantly.

'You can't spend the rest of your life trying to please your mother.'

'I know that,' she said a little sharply. It was something that she had told herself dozens of times, but it was still a habit that was very hard to break.

'Perhaps you should stop right now,' he suggested.

'How?'

A faint grin touched the corners of Lyndon's mouth. 'You could begin by taking home someone quite disreputable—like me.'

'Are you disreputable?'

'Some people seem to think so.'

'They're probably right! Just look at the way you've behaved the last few days. Dragging me here, making me share an apartment with you, and then trying to——' She rather hastily stopped at that point.

'Trying to make love to you?' Lyndon finished, the amusement clear in his voice now. 'But I haven't made any serious attempt at that, yet. In fact, I think I've been extremely well-behaved, in the circumstances.'

'Well-behaved?' Mae gave a small snort. 'But you tried to—I mean, you——' She began to flounder a little there, not quite having the nerve to say it out loud.

'I kissed you,' Lyndon said calmly. 'It was nice, but it didn't have anything to do with making love. If you think that it did, then you're even more inexperienced than I thought.'

'I'm not *that* inexperienced,' Mae said defensively. 'And you didn't just kiss me. You touched me,' she reminded him in a more accusing tone.

'It was really no more than a friendly gesture,' he told her.

She remembered how his fingers had slid over the softness of her breast. First, she blushed; then, she bristled. 'A *very* friendly gesture!'

'I'm a friendly sort of man,' he said easily.

She suddenly realised that they had strayed a long way from their original topic of conversation. Had he done that deliberately? she wondered. To take her mind off that disturbing encounter with Malcolm Morgan? A short while ago, she wouldn't even have considered that possibility. Now that she knew him better, though, she knew he was quite capable of such thoughtfulness.

They walked on in silence for a while. The villa was out of sight now, which made Mae feel slightly better. She was even beginning to be able to think fairly clearly again.

'How are we going to get off Lindos?' she asked.

'We're not leaving this island,' Lyndon replied calmly. 'Not yet.'

Mae's eyebrows shot up. 'Of course we are. Malcolm Morgan warned us what would happen if we didn't leave. And anyway, I certainly don't want to stay here!'

'I never take any notice of threats,' he said, in that same calm tone. 'And we're staying on Lindos until we've found out the truth.'

'Don't you think that should be *my* decision?' Mae said indignantly.

Lyndon looked at her. 'I think it should be *our* decision.'

That rather threw her off balance. 'Well, I vote against it,' she muttered at last.

He smiled at her. 'You'll change your mind, when you've had time to think about it. You've finished running away from things, Mae. Now that you've started this, you'll see it through to the end.'

She scowled at him. 'You seem very certain that you know what I'm thinking and feeling.'

'Yes, I'm certain,' he agreed, disconcerting her still further. 'But if you're going to ask me how I'm certain, I'd have to admit that I don't know. It's just one of those things that seems to have been happening lately.'

As far as Mae was concerned, far too much seemed to be happening! Most of it, she still didn't understand. And the thing that baffled her most of all was how—and why—she had become so entangled with this man.

She took a quick sideways look at him, and was slightly alarmed by the familiar sight of him. The dark hair, the light blue eyes, the tall, lean body—he might have been around for years, instead of only a few days. He was even beginning to feel familiar when he kissed and touched her. If things could change so much in just days, what would happen if he were around for weeks, or months?

Mae decided that she didn't want to think about that, not now. There were too many other problems to be faced.

'All right,' she said at last, in a low voice, 'if we're not going to run away, then what *are* we going to do?'

'Wait around until we get another opportunity to speak to your father,' Lyndon said decisively. Then he looked at her. 'You still don't like hearing him called that, do you?'

'No, I don't. I'm sure that he is my father, but he certainly doesn't *feel* like my father. He's just a stranger,' she burst out.

'And he might always be a stranger,' Lyndon warned. 'Can you cope with that?'

'I suppose I'll have to,' she said, after a few moments' hesitation.

'I think you'll cope,' Lyndon said confidently. 'And if you do hit a bad patch, I'll be around to help you through it.'

Somehow, Mae found that just as alarming as the prospect of meeting Malcolm Morgan again. She chewed her lip, and wondered how this was all going to end.

They walked on a little further, and then Mae came to a sudden halt.

'I'm hot and I'm tired,' she said in an edgy voice. 'Are we just going to walk around the island all day?'

'No,' said Lyndon. 'We need to find somewhere to spend the night. Probably the best place to sleep would be the beach.'

'The beach?' echoed Mae, with a total lack of enthusiasm.

'As long as it doesn't rain, we should be fine. And rain's fairly rare around here at this time of the year.'

'With our luck, there'll probably be a freak storm,' she said gloomily.

Lyndon merely grinned, took hold of her hand, and began to pull her along a narrow track that meandered down to the beach. They were on the south side of the island now, where the coastline was much gentler. There weren't any of the high cliffs that surrounded Malcolm Morgan's villa, and the walk down to the beach was an easy one.

It was late afternoon by the time they reached the beach. Mae flopped down on to the warm sand and closed her aching eyes. She decided that this was beginning to feel like the longest day of her entire life! First, that visit to the cavern, with its awesome stalactites and stalagmites. Then the return to the villa, and more of Lyndon's disturbing kisses. And, finally, Malcolm Morgan walking in, right in the middle of that intimate scene. She gave a small shiver. Why had he chosen *that* moment to make an appearance? She had felt embarrassed, confused and vulnerable all at the same time—not a pleasant experience!

'Tired?' asked Lyndon, sitting beside her.

She opened her eyes with an effort. 'Too much has happened today,' she muttered.

'Try and sleep for an hour,' he advised. 'I'm going back to the villa, to collect our luggage.'

She was immediately more wide awake. 'You're not going to try and see Malcolm Morgan again, are you?'

'He doesn't need to see me,' Lyndon replied. 'He needs to see *you*. But not today,' he added, to her relief. 'It can wait until tomorrow. You need to get some rest first.' He got to his feet. 'I won't be long. Will you be all right on your own?'

'Believe it or not, I can get along without you for an hour or two,' she said with a touch of the old sarcasm.

As usual, he didn't take offence. 'I know you can,' he said with a grin. 'Although I wish that you couldn't! You're surprisingly independent when you put your mind to it, though. My guess is that you've changed a lot during these last few days.'

He turned away and walked back up the beach, leaving Mae to mull over his last few words. She slowly realised that he was right. She *had* changed. Was it because of Lyndon? she wondered uneasily. Or would it have happened anyway? She rather thought that it wouldn't. She doubted if she would ever have summoned up enough nerve to come this far on her own.

She closed her eyes again, and gave a small sigh. Perhaps Lyndon was right, and she should try to get some sleep. The next couple of days promised to put even more of a strain on her overstretched nerves.

She only dozed, though, waking up with a small start a couple of times and wondering dazedly where she was. Finally, she drifted into a slightly deeper sleep, but something woke her up again only minutes later.

It was Lyndon returning. He hadn't made a sound or made any effort to wake her up. She had just responded instinctively to his nearness, opening her eyes as he approached.

He was carrying their luggage, which he dumped in the shade of a nearby outcrop of rock.

'Mrs Matthews seems to be on our side. She's packed us some food, more than enough to see us through until tomorrow, and my guess is that she'll give us more, if we need it.'

'That's because you've charmed her,' Mae pointed out. 'I bet you charm every single woman you meet!'

'Do I charm you?' He tossed the question at her fairly casually, but he seemed to be waiting a little tensely for her reply.

'Of course you don't,' she said at once, but there was very little conviction in her voice.

Lyndon gave her an odd look. 'Sometimes, I wonder if you're ever going to tell me the truth.'

'I always tell the truth,' she insisted firmly.

'You often bend the truth a little,' he said drily, 'and there's a great deal that you never actually say at all.'

Mae was about to make a defensive retort, but instead shut up. She was too tired for this kind of conversation. It would be all too easy to say something she didn't mean, and that would be a bad mistake.

Instead, she turned away from Lyndon and stared out to sea. The sun was setting in a magnificent blaze of colour, and there was still a lot of warmth in its dying rays. Once full darkness fell, though, she knew there would be a chill in the air. Sleeping on the beach

might sound very romantic, but she guessed the reality
was going to be distinctly uncomfortable.

'Want something to eat?' offered Lyndon.

She nodded, glad of the change of subject. He
opened one of the bags, and began to pull out neatly
wrapped parcels. 'Sandwiches, cold pastries, home-
made cake, fresh fruit and a couple of bottles of
mineral water,' he said, laying everything out neatly
on a nearby slab of rock. 'Help yourself.'

Despite everything that had happened, and the
tiredness that still weighed down her limbs and eyes,
Mae realised she was very hungry. She ate a half-share
of everything Lyndon had brought with him, drank
a bottle of mineral water, and then sat back with a
small sigh of contentment. Lyndon had eaten as much
as she had, and there was very little left of the food
Mrs Matthews had packed for them.

'I think you're going to have to go and charm her
all over again tomorrow,' Mae commented. Then she
wrinkled her nose as she rubbed her hands together.
'My fingers are sticky.'

'The washing facilities around here are fairly
limited,' said Lyndon. 'You'll just have to dunk them
in the sea. In fact, all the facilities are limited,' he
said, with a grin. 'Luckily, there are a couple of large
bushes nearby. They're thick enough to offer some
privacy.'

The light was beginning to fade now. Mae rummaged around in her case for the one thick jumper
she had brought with her. It was still quite warm at
the moment, but she guessed she would need it later.

By the time full darkness had closed in around
them, she had had a quick wash in the sea, and used
some of the mineral water to clean her teeth. She

pulled her case over to use as a pillow, and gave a grimace as she settled down on the sand.

'It's a pity Mrs Matthews couldn't have come up with blankets and a pillow, as well as something to eat!'

'I'll work on it tomorrow, if you like,' replied Lyndon, still sitting with his back propped against a nearby rock.

Mae glanced round a little uneasily. The beach at night looked very different from the sunlit place it was during the day. A faint light came from the moon and the stars, but there were still an awful lot of black shadows, and she kept hearing odd noises that she hadn't noticed before.

'This place is spooky,' she muttered.

Lyndon shrugged. 'It's just a beach.'

'Well, I'm used to sleeping in a bed, with a roof over my head! I'm not used to sleeping rough.'

'Stick close to me, and I can promise you a whole lot more new experiences,' he said slyly.

Mae threw a black look at him, although it was probably wasted because it was too dark for him to see it. 'I've had enough new experiences to last me for a lifetime. When this is all over, I'm going back to my dull, ordinary life, and I'm going to love every minute of it.'

'No, you won't. You'll look back on these few days we've spent together, and you'll realise that you've actually enjoyed most of it.'

She stared at him in amazement. 'You don't really think I've *enjoyed* any of this, do you? Sleeping on a beach, being thrown out of people's houses, not knowing from one minute to another what's going to happen next? I liked my life the way it was before!'

'I don't think that you did,' Lyndon replied calmly. 'This is a lot more fun.'

'Fun?' she repeated incredulously. 'How on earth can you call this fun?'

'Oh, there have been parts of it that haven't been too good,' he admitted. 'But we've been able to spend a lot of time together, and we certainly know each other a lot better than we did when we first got on that plane to Athens.'

'I never said that I *wanted* to know you,' Mae pointed out stiffly.

'No, you didn't,' he agreed. 'In fact, you've fought it tooth and nail. I expected that, though. You've been on your own for too long to let anyone into your life without a struggle.'

'I have not been on my own,' she denied indignantly. 'I've got friends, I've had boyfriends——'

'But not many,' he reminded her.

She was about to insist that there had been plenty, but then stopped. There wasn't much point in lying to him. He had done all that damned research into her background! He knew far too much of the truth about her.

Mae subsided into a sulky silence. She was losing this battle of words. She also had the feeling that she was losing a lot of other battles, as well. She didn't like that. It put her in a very vulnerable position.

'I'm going to sleep,' she muttered, closing her eyes so that she could blot out the sight of him sitting there, relaxed and just a little too close for comfort.

'Goodnight, Mae,' he said, with clear amusement in his voice.

She gave a small, annoyed grunt, and then turned over, so that she had her back to him.

Although she hadn't expected to, in just a few minutes exhaustion rolled over her, and she fell asleep. She didn't wake up again until some time later, opening her eyes to find it was still dark. She blinked dozily, and wondered what time it was. The early hours of the morning, she guessed.

She shifted uncomfortably. The sand felt hard and lumpy beneath her, and she was stiff and rather cold. She wasn't cut out for this sort of thing, she decided irritably. She needed a soft bed, clean sheets, and a roof over her head.

After a couple of attempts to find a more comfortable position, she gave up. Then she shivered. Despite pulling on her jumper before she had gone to sleep, she was still cold. It was surprising how chilly the nights could become, after the blazing heat of the day had faded away.

'Having trouble getting back to sleep?' Lyndon's voice, floating out of the darkness, made her jump a little. She hadn't realised he was awake.

'Anyone would have trouble sleeping on this cold, hard beach,' she grumbled.

'There are far worse places where we could have bedded down for the night.'

'Then why are *you* still awake?' she demanded.

His tone was much drier this time, as he answered her. 'When a man can't sleep, the cause is usually a woman.'

'Are you telling me that I'm keeping you awake at nights?' Mae said disbelievingly.

'You sound as if you think that's quite impossible.'

Although she couldn't see his face clearly in the darkness, she knew that he was smiling.

'Of course it's impossible,' she muttered. 'I'm not the type to keep anyone awake.'

'Why do you think that?'

'Well—I just know I'm not,' she said, definitely flustered now.

Lyndon got up, and her heart gave a sudden hard thump as he walked over, and then settled himself beside her.

'Why didn't you stay where you were?' she asked in a voice that showed an irritating tendency to quaver.

'I like being close to you,' he replied calmly.

'How close?' she said suspiciously.

'Close enough to keep you warm. You are cold, aren't you?'

'No!' she lied at once. 'I'm fine. I——' She didn't get a chance to say anything more, because Lyndon had stretched himself out beside her. The long line of his body curved against hers, and Mae very nearly stopped breathing.

'What—what are you doing?' she stuttered.

'Nothing very alarming,' he replied lazily. 'This is a good way for the two of us to keep warm. Relax. Go back to sleep.'

Relax? With just about every inch of him in close contact with her own tense body?

'I think——' Mae gulped hard, and tried again. 'I think you should move away.'

'Why?'

'Well—you can't be enjoying this very much,' she babbled. 'You told me once that you always slept alone. That you didn't like sleeping with anyone else.'

'I'm prepared to make an exception in your case,' he told her.

'All the same, this isn't—I mean, I don't want—you shouldn't——'

'Stop chattering. You're keeping me awake.'

She was keeping *him* awake? If he didn't move, then she wasn't going to get a single wink of sleep all night!

Cautiously, she began to edge away from him. If he wouldn't move, then she was the one who would have to find another sleeping-place.

Lyndon's arm immediately came over her, stopping her from going any further. 'Lie still,' he instructed.

With the heavy weight of his arm pinning her down, she didn't have very much choice. And she didn't dare struggle any further. That would mean they could end up in even closer contact, and who knew where that might lead? At least he seemed content just to lie beside her—for the moment.

Mae licked her dry lips. It felt very funny to be curled up alongside him, like this. Funny, but not altogether unpleasant. In fact, she had the rather alarming feeling that she could very easily get used to it; even begin to like it.

Go to sleep, she told herself, with a touch of panic. Forget he's even there. Pretend you're curled up beside a couple of pillows, not the warm, hard body of a man!

Except that took an effort of imagination that was just beyond her. No matter how much she tried, she couldn't pretend that Lyndon Alexander Hyde was a pillow!

After about half an hour, when nothing at all alarming had happened and Lyndon hadn't made the slightest effort to take things any further, she finally began to relax just a little. A few minutes later, she closed her eyes. And soon after that, with a small sigh, she fell asleep.

CHAPTER EIGHT

WHEN Mae woke up again, the sun was shining, the chill of the night had already disappeared, and there was no sign of Lyndon.

Nervously, she sat up and looked around. Where had he gone? Then she told herself that she was being ridiculous. Last night, she had been totally on edge because he had been far too close. Now, her nerves were twitching because she couldn't see him!

She pulled off her jumper, feeling too warm as the sun steadily gained in heat. Then she ran her fingers through her tangled red curls, trying to restore them to some kind of order.

When she looked up again, she realised that she could finally see Lyndon. He was some way out to sea, but swimming strongly and steadily back towards the shore.

'Coming in?' he called out, when he was within earshot.

'No,' Mae said firmly. She wasn't in the mood for frolicking around in the water with anyone, and especially not with Lyndon.

'Then I'll come out,' he said.

He began to wade towards the beach, and at the last moment Mae remembered that he hadn't brought any swimming-trunks with him. She hastily began to close her eyes, but it was already too late. Lyndon was almost out of the water.

Then she gave a small sigh of relief as she realised that he was wearing a pair of pants. He reached for the towel he had left draped over a nearby rock, quickly dried himself, and then pulled on a T-shirt.

'I can't put on my jeans until my pants are dry,' he said with a grin. 'But at least I'm halfway decent.' He stretched out on the sand, to finish drying off, and looked up at her through half-closed eyes. 'Sleep well?' he asked.

'Yes, thank you,' Mae said stiffly.

'So did I. That rather surprised me,' he said equably. 'I didn't expect to sleep at all.'

Mae didn't know quite what to say, and so she kept quiet. Lyndon closed his eyes and seemed to doze, and everything remained unexpectedly peaceful for the next half-hour.

By the time Lyndon opened his eyes again, she had washed and put on clean clothes. He yawned, stretched, and then pulled on his jeans. Mae was rather relieved about that. There had been something distinctly distracting about the sight of his bare, strongly muscled legs!

'What are we going to do this morning?' she asked, as he slid his feet into a pair of sandals.

'We're going to talk to your father again,' he replied in a calm voice.

Mae's nerves instantly gave a hefty twitch. 'I don't think that's a very good idea. Anyway, how *can* we see him? He isn't just going to open the door and invite us in!'

'We'll see him,' Lyndon said with confidence. 'I'll find a way of bringing the two of you together.'

'Perhaps we could leave it until tomorrow,' Mae suggested hopefully.

'We'll go today,' Lyndon told her firmly. 'And don't worry,' he said with a sudden smile. 'Everything will turn out all right.'

'I think you've told me that before,' she said, throwing a dark look at him. 'But so far, nothing seems to be turning out very well at all!'

'I wouldn't say that,' he replied equably. 'Things seem to be going particularly well between the two of us at the moment. And we've just spent a very pleasant night together,' he reminded her, with a grin that was quite deliberately wicked.

'I don't want to hear one more word about last night!' she warned him fiercely. Then she snatched up her case. 'All right, let's go to see Malcolm Morgan.'

During the walk to Malcolm Morgan's villa, though, Mae had plenty of time for second thoughts. Perhaps seeing him again wasn't such a good idea. In fact, just the thought of it made her extremely nervous.

'What if he simply throws us out?' she said edgily.

'He won't,' Lyndon said, with some conviction. 'And don't be scared. Whether he's your father or not, there's no need to be afraid of him.'

'That's easy for you to say!' she retorted. 'You're not afraid of anyone.'

'There are times when *you* scare me half to death,' he said, to her total astonishment.

She stopped dead and stared at him. *'Me?'*

'You're threatening to change my life in ways I never thought were possible,' he said, with an odd smile. 'I liked my life the way it was. It suited me. Now, the future's a lot more uncertain. More responsibilities, having to consider another person as well as myself, probably less freedom and independence, but a lot of other things that will more than compensate for that. If I stopped to think about what I was taking on, I might well find it quite terrifying.'

She found she was a little breathless, even though she was standing quite still. 'You don't have to take on anything at all,' she mumbled at last.

He gave an easy shrug. 'I don't think I've got very much choice.' Then he gave her a gentle push. 'Let's keep walking. I want to get to the villa fairly early, in case Malcolm Morgan decides to take off in his yacht again.'

That distracted Mae from what he had said to her previously. 'Do you really think he'd do that?'

'I should think that he's beginning to feel rather nervous about seeing you again. He might not want to face you.'

'I'm making *him* nervous?' she said incredulously.

'Why not?' said Lyndon. 'He's had time to think about his meeting with you, time to realise how very much you look like him. There must be at least a small note of doubt in his mind by now.'

They began to walk on, and, just minutes later, the villa came into view. Mae gulped hard as she saw it. If Lyndon hadn't been beside her, she would almost certainly have turned and run away.

They went through the front entrance, but there was no sign of either Malcolm Morgan or Mrs Matthews, the housekeeper.

'What do we do?' asked Mae shakily. 'Knock at the front door?'

'There's no need for that,' said Lyndon. He was looking over the edge of the terrace, at the bay below. 'He's down on the beach. He's probably been working on his yacht. We'll go down to meet him,' he added decisively.

Mae clung tightly to Lyndon's hand as they began to make their way down the steep steps that led to the beach. And it wasn't only because the climb made her head swim dizzily. Malcolm Morgan spotted them when they were only halfway down, and, by the time they reached the bottom of the steps, he was standing waiting for them, his yellow eyes blazing angrily.

'I told you what would happen if you didn't get off this island,' he told them grimly. Then he glared at Lyndon. 'And I know who you are now. You're the reporter who's been digging into my background. I was warned a couple of weeks ago that someone had been asking a lot of questions. And some personal files have been tampered with. Once I can prove that you were responsible for that, you'll be facing criminal charges!'

'And would you really enjoy the publicity that would follow, if all of this ended up in a court of law?' Lyndon asked quietly.

'No, I wouldn't. But, by heaven, I'd sooner face that than give in to blackmail!'

'What do you mean, blackmail?' Mae jumped in hotly.

Malcolm Morgan's gaze swept over her with open contempt. 'That's what this is all about, isn't it? Money? Your boyfriend here is going to write an article about me for some grubby little rag. And if I don't pay you enough money, then that article will contain a lot of sensational revelations about my "long-lost daughter". Not a word of it will be true, of course, but people don't care about that, do they?

They just like to read about the dirt in other people's lives. And you're going to produce that dirt!'

Mae put her hand on Lyndon's arm. 'It's no use talking to him,' she said quietly. 'Let's go.'

Lyndon didn't move, though. Instead, his light blue gaze fixed on Malcolm Morgan's face. 'Firstly,' he said in a voice that was just a little too calm, 'not one word about Mae will appear in any article I ever write. Secondly, neither of us are interested in a single penny of your money. And, thirdly, if you let Mae walk out of your life, then it will be your loss, not hers.'

At that, Malcolm Morgan's eyes narrowed. 'Mae?' he said sharply. 'Is this girl Mae Stanfield? Margaret Stanfield's daughter?' Then he seemed to realise that he had said too much, and he abruptly stopped.

'That's right,' Lyndon said softly. 'This is the girl whose schooling you paid for. Whose medical bills you paid.'

Mae found she was holding her breath. The very air seemed to shimmer with a dangerous tension, as if the situation could explode into sudden violence at any moment.

'Very clever,' Malcolm Morgan said slowly, at last. 'You didn't find just any red-haired, yellow-eyed girl. You found Margaret Stanfield's daughter. You're a cleverer man than I thought, Mr Hyde. But then, you're playing for extremely high stakes, aren't you?'

Mae somehow found her voice. 'We've already told you that we're not interested in your money.'

'And I don't believe you,' Malcolm Morgan said harshly. 'Everyone's interested in money, especially when there's such a large amount of it at stake.'

Mae ignored that. 'Then you did know my mother?' she said in a shaky voice.

'Yes, I knew her,' he said, after a short pause. 'There was a time when we were—very close.'

She bit her lip. 'Then it's—it's not impossible that I'm your daughter?' she somehow managed to get out.

Malcolm Morgan's eyes remained cold. 'I'm afraid that it's totally impossible, Miss Stanfield. When your mother told me she was pregnant, I knew that she'd been sleeping with someone else. I threw her out, just the way I'm going to throw you out.'

'If you're so certain Mae isn't your child, why did you pay her school and medical bills?' cut in Lyndon.

'Because I was once very fond of her mother,' he said grudgingly. 'And, despite the fact that she deceived me, I rather regretted the way the affair ended. Some very harsh and cruel things were said—mostly by me. Paying for her child's schooling and for private hospital treatment when she needed it was a way of making amends.'

'In other words, it salved your conscience!' Mae said heatedly.

He gave a small shrug. 'If you want to put it that way—yes.'

'And you still won't accept that the child her mother had was *your* child?' Lyndon challenged him.

Malcolm Morgan's face changed again. Now there was a growing anger behind his eyes. 'I've already told you that isn't possible.'

'But you haven't told us why,' Mae said, looking straight at him. 'And I *need* to know why.'

Yellow eyes met yellow eyes, and for just a moment something seemed to pass between them. Then Malcolm Morgan looked away, his face darkening.

'I've had three wives, and a great many casual affairs, but I've no children,' he muttered at last. 'And there's a very good reason for that. I'm infertile! I've been to every top specialist in the field, had endless tests, and been told the same thing every time. My chances of fathering a child are less than one in a million. And I don't believe in those sort of odds.'

Mae swallowed hard, and even Lyndon was silent for several moments. Then his blue gaze returned to Malcolm Morgan's face.

'But what if that chance in a million did finally come up?' he said quietly. 'I'm sure Mae would be willing to take a blood test, to prove it one way or another.'

Malcolm Morgan looked at Mae again. He couldn't seem to take his eyes off her dark red hair, her yellow eyes, so like his own.

'Your mother was the only woman in my life I really cared for,' he said at last, in an odd voice. Then he stopped and gave a deep scowl. Mae felt her stomach muscles knot. It was exactly the way *she* scowled when she was highly disturbed about something. 'I need to think about this,' he muttered at last. 'Go away and leave me alone. Come back later. But on your own,' he instructed, looking directly at Mae.

Lyndon took her by the hand and gently pulled her away. 'Let's go,' he said softly.

She climbed the steps in a daze. When they finally reached the top, she turned to Lyndon.

'If he's starting to believe that I might—just might—be his daughter, why did he send me away?'

'He just wants some time on his own,' Lyndon told her. 'If you really are his daughter, then it's going to turn his life completely upside-down. More than that, he's going to have to accept that he treated your mother quite appallingly. Obviously, he refused to believe her when she told him she was having his child, and threw her out. If he made a mistake—and I'm absolutely certain that he did—then he's going to find that a very hard thing to live with.'

'No wonder my mother would never talk about him,' said Mae, in a low voice. 'She must have absolutely hated him for the way he treated her. And yet she took money from him,' she said in a puzzled tone. 'How could she do that, after what he'd done to her?'

'She didn't take the money for herself,' Lyndon pointed out. 'Only for you. She must have reasoned that you were entitled to it, since you were his child.' He looked at her. 'Are you going back to see him later?'

'I suppose so,' she said reluctantly. 'Now that I've come this far, I can't just turn tail and run.' She gave him a rueful smile. 'You've taught me that it's no good running away from things.'

He studied her face. 'I wonder what else I've taught you,' he said softly.

But Mae didn't want to answer that question right now. Her head was still whirling. There were so many changes in her life to cope with, and not enough time to come to terms with them all.

Just at that moment, rather to her relief, Mrs Matthews came bustling out of the villa. 'Would you like to come in and have some lunch? she asked.

Lyndon lifted one eyebrow. 'Will Mr Morgan approve?'

'Probably not,' she said briskly. 'But good housekeepers are very hard to find. I don't think he'll risk firing me just because I've given the two of you a meal.'

Mae trailed after them into the villa, but could only pick at the food on her plate when it was finally placed in front of her. She was going to have to face Malcolm Morgan again later—and on her own. He might be her father—he almost certainly *was* her father—but she wasn't looking forward to it one little bit.

After they had eaten, Mrs Matthews left them on their own. They sat in silence for a while. Then Lyndon looked at her.

'I think it's time you went and saw him,' he said quietly.

'I want you to come with me.' She hadn't meant to say any such thing, but the words just burst out of her.

Lyndon shook his head, though. 'This is something that you've got to do on your own. I'll wait here for you.'

'Please,' she pleaded.

'No.' His voice was gentle, but very firm. 'I've brought you as far as I can. You've got to take this last step by yourself.'

She knew he was right. That didn't make it any easier, though. She got up on stiff, tense legs, and walked slowly towards the door. When she got there, she looked back at Lyndon. His blue eyes rested on her for a long moment and he gave her a slow smile. That somehow gave her the courage to keep going, out of the villa and down the steep steps, to meet Malcolm Morgan—to meet her father.

He was waiting for her on the beach, sitting on a rock and staring out to sea. She walked right up to him before he turned his head and looked at her. Then he gave a brief nod.

'I thought you'd come.'

'What do you want to say to me?' she asked steadily.

'That's a good question,' he said rather gruffly. 'What can I say, after all these years? That I'm sorry? That seems rather inadequate.'

Mae took a very deep breath. 'Then you do think there's a chance I might be your daughter? You'd be willing for us to take blood tests, to find out for certain?'

He was silent for a very long time. 'I don't need any blood tests to tell me the truth,' he said at last. 'There's no way Margaret Stanfield could have had a child by another man, and yet that same child grew up to look so much like me. Your mother was telling me the truth all along. Much too late in the day, I finally believe her.' He raised his head. 'Did your mother at last tell you about me? Is that how you found out who I was?'

'She's never mentioned your name,' Mae said steadily. 'I used to ask her about my father when I was younger, but she would just turn away from me and refuse to discuss it.'

'She must loathe and despise me,' he said a little thickly.

'Yes, I think that she does.'

There was another long silence from Malcolm Morgan. Then he looked up at her again. 'If your mother didn't tell you about me, how did you find me?'

'I didn't. It was Lyndon who worked it out, Lyndon who brought me here.'

'Ah, yes,' he said softly. 'The clever Mr Hyde.'

There was something about his tone of voice that immediately put Mae on her guard.

'Yes, he's clever,' she said defensively. 'He's also helped me a great deal over the past few days.'

'Of course he has. The question is, why? Or are you going to tell me that your Mr Hyde has done all this out of pure charity?'

'Why are we talking about Lyndon?' Mae asked with a puzzled frown. 'Surely there are more important things we should be discussing?'

Malcolm Morgan looked hard at her. 'If you are my daughter—and it looks as if I'm going to have to believe that you are—then there are several things that you're going to have to learn fairly fast. And the first—and most important—is that you'll have to choose your friends a lot more carefully in the future.'

She straightened her shoulders, not at all liking the way this conversation was going. 'What exactly do you mean by that?'

'Isn't it fairly obvious?' His yellow eyes, so like her own, fixed steadily on her. 'People are going to want to know you, get close to you, because of who you are.'

She looked back at him with growing hostility. 'Do you mean Lyndon?' she challenged him directly. 'If you do, I don't know how you can say such a thing. You don't know anything about him.'

'Yes, I do,' Malcolm Morgan said softly. 'I've had my people doing some research into his background.'

'Why?' she said sharply.

'He's been prying into my life, so I've made it my business to find out something about his. Let's just say that I was very interested to find out why he's gone to so much trouble to reunite me with my long-lost daughter. And why he's obviously made such an effort to get *close* to my daughter. Mr Hyde is a very attractive man,' he went on, ignoring the small flush of heat that had begun to spread over Mae's face. 'Men like that can usually have any woman they choose. So, the question is—why has he picked you?'

'I don't think I want to talk about this any more,' Mae said in a stiff voice.

'Well, I do. For a start, I'd be interested to hear just how much you know about Mr Lyndon Hyde.'

'He's a journalist,' Mae said defensively. 'He works for a quality paper, not the gutter Press. And he isn't married, if that's what you're thinking. He lives alone, in a flat in central London.'

'He lives in a very *expensive* flat,' Malcolm Morgan corrected her. 'And he drives a luxury car. How do you suppose he pays for that kind of lifestyle, Mae?' She didn't want to admit that she didn't know, and so she stayed silent. 'I can tell you where the money came from,' he went on. 'A couple of years ago, using a pseudonym, he wrote a very successful novel, a political thriller. The film rights were taken up, which brought in even more money, and Mr Hyde found himself with a great deal of cash in his hands, which he seems to have spent very freely. No more books followed, though. It seems that he was a one-book wonder. And now the money's beginning to run out. The royalties are still trickling in, of course, but only in fairly small amounts. Soon, they'll begin to dry up completely. A topical thriller sells well at the time, but has a fairly limited lifespan. My Hyde's very comfortable lifestyle is about to come to an end. The expensive flat and the car will both have to go—unless he finds some other source of income.'

Mae's throat had become rather dry. 'He has a good job,' she argued. 'He certainly won't starve.'

'No, he won't starve,' agreed Malcolm Morgan. 'But he's become used to the good things in life. It's very hard to give them up, once you've developed a taste for them.'

'I really don't know why you're telling me all this,' she said in a prickly tone.

'Of course you do. You just don't want to face facts.'

'What facts?' she demanded hotly.

'That Mr Hyde is out to make the most of an amazing piece of good luck. He began to do some research for an article on a very wealthy and powerful man, and turned up some information that he found extremely interesting. I've already said that Mr Hyde is clever, and he is. He put all the facts together, and came up with the startling conclusion that this man had a daughter that he didn't even know about.'

'Any first-class journalist could have reached the same conclusion,' Mae retorted.

'Yes, they could,' Malcolm Morgan agreed. 'But only an opportunist like Lyndon Hyde would use that information for his own ends.'

Mae's eyes flashed fiercely. 'You'd better explain exactly what you mean by that!'

'It's very simple. Lyndon Hyde decided that you could provide him with a golden opportunity to improve his own future. All he had to do was to make you fall in love with him. And for a man like him, that presented no problems. He's an expert, where women are concerned. I recognised the type at once. Once you *were* in love with him, his future was secure. A quick wedding, to make the whole thing legal, and then he would be in line for a very nice share of my considerable wealth. He knew very well I had no other children. No one else to share my money with—no one else to leave it to, when I finally died. Mr Lyndon Hyde had found himself a very nice little gold mine.'

'That is a disgusting thing to say!' Mae said in a low, trembling voice. 'Anyway, what if it turned out I *wasn't* your daughter? He didn't know for certain, when we started out.'

'The odds were on his side, though,' Malcolm Morgan replied in a dispassionate tone. 'And my guess is that there's been no talk of wedding bells, yet. He wanted to wait and make quite sure first that I'd accept you as my child. And if the whole thing turned out to be a huge mistake, then he could simply dump you and go back to his old life.'

Mae had almost forgotten by now that this man was her father. Someone she had wondered about, dreamt about, all of her life.

'Perhaps you shouldn't judge everyone by your own standards!' she threw back at him angrily.

'And perhaps *you* should stop being so naïve,' he answered, an edge to his own voice now. 'Grow up, start seeing things the way they really are. This man moved in on you, Mae. You don't strike me as a stupid girl, you must be able to see that for yourself. He planned the whole thing right from the very beginning. He wanted you, because he thought you could provide him with the very comfortable lifestyle that he's developed such a taste for. And now he's got you—unless you've got the guts to tell him to get the hell out of your life.'

They stood staring at each other, yellow gaze locked to yellow gaze. Then Mae somehow managed to wrench her eyes away.

'I think I'm beginning to understand now why my mother would never talk about you,' she said in disgust. 'Why she wouldn't even tell me your name.'

With that, she turned her back on him and ran quickly up the steep steps that led back to the villa. She didn't look back, even once, at the man on the beach. She tried not even to think about him—and what he had said—although that was very much harder.

Lyndon was waiting for her on the terrace. He took one look at her face; then he gripped her arm and steered her into the small apartment at the back of the villa.

Once they were inside, he closed the door and locked it. 'What happened?' he said abruptly.

Mae looked around a little dazedly, rather belatedly realising where they were.

'We shouldn't be here,' she muttered.

'Never mind about that. What did Malcolm Morgan say to you?'

But she didn't want to tell him. She didn't want to repeat that conversation to anyone, and especially not to Lyndon.

He gave her a none too gentle shake. 'Mae, talk to me! What did he say?'

She raised her eyes to his, and shivered a little when she saw the fierce light in them. Then she began gabbling too fast, as if all the words pent-up inside of her needed to pour out in a cleansing torrent.

'He kept talking about *you*. Not about me, or my mother, or the past. Just about you. About why you'd brought me here, what you were like, why you wanted me. He knew all about you, about that book you wrote, all that money and how you'd spent it. And he said now the money was running out, but you wanted more, and you'd found a way to get it. He said——' Her voice finally trembled to a halt. And when she lifted her gaze to Lyndon again, he looked so angry that she hardly recognised him.

'I get it,' he said tightly. 'According to him, you're my ticket back to the good life. I want you because of who you are—Malcolm Morgan's daughter. I want you because, once I've got you, there's a good chance I might also be able to get my hands on some of his money.' She nodded numbly. 'Well, let me tell you something,' he went on in the same taut voice. 'There *was* a time when I wanted money. When I quite deliberately set out to make as much of it as I could. I wrote a book that I knew would sell well if I could get enough promotion and publicity, and when they jumped at the film rights I was sure I had it made. The money began to roll in, and I thought I'd finally begun to make a success of my life. It was what I had wanted, I was convinced it was going to make up for all the other things that had been lacking in my life. A proper family, a decent childhood, love and attention from people who really cared about me.' Then his face suddenly twisted into a painful grimace. 'Only I soon found out that it didn't make up for those things at all. All the success and money in the world couldn't give me the things I really wanted. That came as quite a shock! It also made me re-evaluate my life. I gave up plans to write a second book, and went back to the one thing that I really enjoyed and gave me satisfaction—journalism.'

Mae's eyes fixed on his face. 'You really don't care about the money?'

'On its own, money is useless,' he said abruptly. 'It took me just a few months to find that out.' Then his blue eyes flared. 'Do you believe me? Or do you think your father's right, and I'm only interested in you because I want to get my hands on his fortune?'

Mae didn't hesitate before replying. 'I believe you.'

His face was still set into tense lines, though. 'Then prove it to me,' he said, his blue gaze seeming to bore right into her. 'Commit yourself to me.'

'How?'

'Sleep with me. Right now.'

She knew the shock was clear in her eyes. 'I—I've already told you that I believe you,' she stammered. 'I d-don't need to sleep with you.'

'But perhaps *I* need it,' he told her in a rough tone. There was a hungry look sweeping over his dark features now. Mae saw it and something inside her shivered. She had never seen him in this sort of mood before. It was as if he was showing her a side of himself that he normally kept hidden from the world. A side that had its roots in his deprived childhood and still haunted him in his adult life. It had made him into a man who lacked something vital in his life, and, now that he had a chance of finding it, he wanted to grasp it greedily and hold on to it.

She looked around a little desperately. 'Not here,' she whispered. 'Not in *this* house.'

'Yes, here,' Lyndon insisted tersely, 'under your father's roof.'

Suddenly, Mae knew why he wanted it to be here. He needed to know that he was more important than anyone in her life, even her newly found father. A small part of him was still the unloved child that he had once been, desperately wanting someone to care about *him* above everyone else.

He was shaking a little now with the need that was running through him with increasing force, but he wouldn't take a step towards her or make the first move. Mae knew that the decision was going to have to be hers.

She licked her suddenly dry lips. Then she rather timidly reached out her hand and touched him.

It was all he needed to break down the rigid self-control that he had imposed on himself. With one short stride, he was beside her. A second later, Mae found herself drowning under a kiss that was fiercely intense and possessive.

Other kisses followed, deep and dark and just a little unnerving in their intensity. There was no time to catch any more than an occasional ragged snatch of breath, or mutter something brief and incoherent.

Then Lyndon finally raised his head for just a second.

'This isn't going to be slow or gentle,' he warned thickly.

'It doesn't matter,' Mae somehow managed to get out. And, amazingly, it was true. She trusted this man implicitly. And anything he did to her would be all right because she would understand *why* he did it. She had passed the point where he was capable of frightening her in any way.

He picked her up and carried her into the bedroom. He paused only to pull down the blind. Then he pushed her a little roughly on to the bed.

'I want to see you naked,' he told her in a husky tone as he stretched out beside her. 'Totally, deliciously naked.'

His hands were already pulling impatiently at her clothes. Mae found herself stretching her limbs and arching her body, so that he could drag them off more quickly. She could hardly believe that she was behaving like this; Mae Stanfield, who had never even particularly enjoyed kissing.

As soon as her breasts were free, his mouth fastened on to them, licking and kissing, and then very gently biting. She let out a small, thick sound of pleasure, and he briefly raised his head and smiled.

'You were made for me,' he told her. 'I knew it from almost the first moment I saw you. And now you're going to be mine for the rest of your life.'

It was a slightly terrifying and yet dizzyingly pleasurable prospect. There was no time to dwell on it, though, because Lyndon was already moving on with almost uncontrollable impatience.

The last of her clothes were torn off, and he allowed himself a couple of seconds just to look at her, his eyes burning very brightly now. Then he dragged in an unsteady breath.

'Beautiful,' he said in a shaky voice. 'Inside and out, you're very beautiful.'

His fingers brushed against the silky warmth of her thighs, and she was trembling even more than he was by now. Never in her life had she felt like this—even known it was *possible* to feel like this. Burning hot and yet shivering deep inside. Too restless to keep still and yet somehow very calm and at peace.

His hands touched and explored, arousing wave after wave of explosive new sensations. He didn't seem to care how intimate his caresses became. Mae caught her breath again, and again, until it seemed impossible to breathe at all.

Lyndon moved yet closer, and she realised that he was still almost fully dressed. She could feel the light rasp of his clothes against the length of her body, the soft cotton of his shirt and the rougher texture of his jeans. Almost instinctively, she began to undo the buttons on his shirt, the zip on his jeans, searching for and finding the hot, supple skin underneath, the hardness of a body that was nearing the very limits of any kind of control. He didn't have to tell her that he liked being touched. She knew it from the tight flexing of his muscles and the faint groan that escaped him.

When she tried to pull his clothes off further, though, aching for the sensation of skin against skin, he caught hold of her hands.

'No time,' he muttered unsteadily. 'I did warn you this wouldn't be slow.'

He was moving over her even as he spoke, gathering her up against him, winding her limbs around him, easing her closer and closer until he was velvet-smooth inside of her, his mouth finding hers at the same time so that deep, drugging kisses accompanied the other, fierce waves of pleasure that swept through her.

Then there was heat and darkness, and a whirlpool of strange, sweet sensations that intensified into a quite cataclysmic eruption of delight. Lyndon's body shuddered in unison, and for a long, long time they seemed to drift downwards on gently decreasing waves of euphoria. Then everything became very still and very quiet, as if the world had actually stopped turning for a while.

Lyndon was the first one to move. He gently eased his weight off her; then he smiled down at her.

'Is this the same girl who once insisted that she didn't like kissing?' he murmured.

Mae slowly began to drift back to reality. 'I didn't know—I didn't think I could——' she began in a rather disorientated voice.

He bent his head and lightly kissed her. 'I think that you're beginning to turn into a rather remarkable woman, Mae Stanfield. And I'm glad that you're going to be *my* woman.'

'I haven't actually said that,' she muttered just a little defensively.

'Oh, yes, you have,' he said, his smile deepening. 'And in just about every way it's possible to say it.'

Mae could feel a flush of heat creeping over her face, and, no matter how hard she tried, she couldn't stop it. Everything had suddenly begun to move much faster than she had expected. And now, she had committed herself in the most positive way possible to Lyndon, and she wasn't even sure what he actually wanted from her. Love? He had never once said that word to her. A long-term relationship? He had certainly hinted at it, but that was all. Nothing definite had been said.

And what did *she* want from *him*? Well, that was easy enough to answer now, she thought with a small grimace. She wanted to stay with him for the rest of her life. Without too much difficulty, he had made her fall totally in love with him.

Whatever kind of future she had from now on was going to depend almost entirely on a man whom she had only known for a few days. Too late, Mae realised that this was the most terrifying—and yet exhilarating—thing that had ever happened to her.

CHAPTER NINE

QUARTER of an hour later, Mae was dressed again. Nothing more had been said between them, but they both understood that they wanted to leave the villa as soon as possible.

As she stepped out into the hot blaze of sunshine outside, Mae still felt as if everything was rather unreal. Then Lyndon turned his head and smiled at her, a slow, intimate smile, and things gradually began to fall into place and make some sort of sense. She had made what was probably the most momentous decision she would ever make, and it was too late now for any misgivings or regrets—not that she had really had any, in the first place. Looking back, she realised that all of this had been fairly inevitable since the day that Lyndon had first made an appearance in her life.

They crossed the terrace, and were just walking towards the open archway that would take them out of the villa when Malcolm Morgan suddenly appeared at the top of the steps that led up from the beach.

His yellow gaze slid over them slowly. Then his eyes rested on Mae and his expression hardened.

'You're leaving?' he said flatly.

'There doesn't seem any reason for her to stay,' Lyndon replied in a calm tone.

Malcolm Morgan ignored him. Instead, he kept looking at Mae.

'I warned you about this man,' he reminded her, his features becoming even more grim. 'He isn't interested in *you*. Why can't you see that? He's only interested in who you are!'

'Yes, he's interested in who I am,' Mae agreed, somehow managing to keep her voice from shaking. 'But to him, I'm Mae Stanfield, not Malcolm Morgan's daughter.'

'If you believe that, then you're a complete fool,' he said harshly. 'And I don't give my money to fools. Stay with him, and you won't ever get a penny from me.'

'Well, I won't be any worse off than I was before,' Mae replied steadily.

'Won't you?' Malcolm Morgan's mouth set into a thin line. 'My guess is that you're going to take it pretty badly when Lyndon Hyde walks out on you, because the money he's been counting on hasn't materialised.'

'I shan't be walking out on anyone,' said Lyndon, and there was a dangerous edge to his tone now.

'You'll hang around for a while, hoping that I'll eventually have a change of heart?' Malcolm Morgan said tersely. 'Forget it! Mae won't get a penny from me while you're around.'

'We don't want or need your money,' said Lyndon, with open disgust. 'All Mae ever wanted was to find her father. I think she's probably deeply regretting that she ever achieved that ambition, though.'

Malcolm Morgan shot a black look at Lyndon. Then he turned back to Mae, and there was a new urgency in his voice, now.

'Stay here, with me,' he said, to her astonishment. 'I can give you everything you'll ever need. If you want to work, I can put you into a top job. If you want to live a life of leisure, I can afford to keep you in a style that you've probably never even dreamed of. You're my child, my only child, turning up like a miracle when I thought I would never have any children at all.'

For a few moments, something tugged deep inside of Mae. She had thought that it would be impossible to feel anything at all for this man who seemed to value money and power above all else, but there *was* something there. His next words snuffed out that small spark of feeling instantly, though.

'I'll pay you to leave her alone,' he grated, turning back to Lyndon. 'I know that I just said you'd never get your hands on my money, but it would be worth it to get rid of you. Sign a legal document stating that you'll never come near her again, and you can name your price.'

Mae could hardly believe she was hearing this. She was about to choke something out, when Lyndon took a step forward.

'I want nothing at all from you,' he said in a soft and yet infinitely dangerous voice. 'I've already got everything that I'll ever want or need. And a biological accident might have made you responsible for Mae's birth, but the best thing you ever did for her was to disown her. No one needs a father like you.'

Malcolm Morgan's face went very white, but he still refused to accept that he couldn't buy the child he had always wanted.

'Let Mae speak for herself,' he ordered. 'I'm offering her the kind of life that you couldn't give her in a million years. Perhaps she's got enough of my blood in her to realise that no one in their right mind would turn down this sort of opportunity.'

At that, Mae lifted her head and looked directly at her father. 'Ever since we first met, just about the only thing you've talked about is money. First of all, you thought I was an imposter out to cheat you. Then you couldn't stop talking about Lyndon and how he was only interested in getting his hands on all your wealth. Not once have you shown any real interest in *me*. You haven't asked me about my childhood, what I like doing, how I earn my living, or whether I'm happy with my life. You haven't asked about my mother, and how she coped all those years bringing up a child on her own.' Her yellow eyes were very bright now, but she blinked fiercely and went on. 'You keep on about my being your child, but I don't really mean anything to you, I'm just a possession. Except that you always thought that this was one possession you would never be able to have, and so that makes me more valuable. You're willing to pay a very high price for me, provided you can have me all to yourself. Well, I'm not for sale!' she finished, brushing her eyes quickly with her hand, so that none of the tears would actually fall. 'Lyndon's right, I don't need a father like you.' She turned to Lyndon. 'I'd like to go now,' she said in a very clear voice.

Immediately, he took hold of her hand and began to lead her out of the villa.

'You're going to regret this!' Malcolm Morgan shouted after them.

Neither of them answered. Instead, they just kept steadily walking until the villa—and Malcolm Morgan—were out of sight.

Once they were a safe distance away, Mae realised that she had to stop for a few minutes. Her legs just wouldn't carry her any further. They sat down on the low wall that ran alongside the narrow road, Lyndon keeping her hand still firmly linked inside his.

'I shouldn't have brought you here,' he said at last. 'I was wrong to interfere in your life the way I did, wrong to make you confront your father. In fact, I think I've been wrong about just about everything.'

Mae looked at him with anxious eyes. 'But not about us?' she said in a rather tremulous voice.

'No, not about us,' he agreed at once, to her relief. 'But I realise now that I was living my dreams through you, which isn't at all a healthy thing to do. Helping you to find your father was a way of compensating for the fact that I was never going to be able to find mine. I shouldn't have done it, I had no right. All that's happened is that you've ended up badly hurt.'

'But at least I know the truth now,' she said, after a long silence. 'Even the way things have turned out, I think I prefer that to knowing nothing at all.' Then she lowered her eyes. 'It's funny, isn't it?' she went on in a rather strained voice. 'I've spent most of my life wondering about my father, drawing mental pictures of him, imagining what he would be like. And now that I've found him—I don't like him. I don't like him one little bit.'

'People who spend their entire lives striving for more and more wealth and power are rarely very likeable,' said Lyndon quietly. Then he gave her a gentle smile. 'What do you want to do now? I think I'll let you make the decisions from now on,' he said drily. 'I don't seem to have made a very good job of it, so far.'

Mae suddenly felt extraordinarily tired. 'I want to go home,' she said. 'Back to England. Can we do that?'

'Mrs Matthews told me earlier that there's a supply boat calling at the island this afternoon. If you can walk as far as the quayside, we can be on it.'

'I'll walk a hundred miles, if it means there's a chance of getting off this island.'

'Half a mile should be enough,' Lyndon said with a faint smile. 'But we'd better start right now. The supply boat only stays here for the time that it takes to unload.'

Mae trudged wearily along beside him, holding on to his hand as if it were some kind of lifeline. She felt totally drained, aware of very little except a numbing sense of exhaustion, and the firm, warm grip of Lyndon's fingers.

When they finally arrived at the quayside, they found the supply boat already moored there. It was skippered by the same tall dark Greek who had brought them to Lindos, and he greeted them with a cheery wave of his hand.

Mae was incapable of responding. She left everything to Lyndon, and simply flopped in a limp heap on the deck.

The long journey back home took on a dreamlike quality after that. She slept much of the time, curled up against Lyndon's shoulder, only dimly aware of the crowds of holiday-makers on the packed ferry, the heat of the sun, and then the contrasting coolness of the plane on the last leg of their journey.

At last, they were back home in England. As they left the airport terminal, Lyndon flagged down a taxi. Mae scrambled in, her eyes still heavy despite all the sleep she had had. Lyndon got in beside her, and then turned to her.

'Where do you want to go?' he asked.

'Back to my flat,' she said without thinking. Then, as she saw the look on his face, she added quickly, 'I need some time on my own. Just a day or two, to rest and to think. You do understand, don't you?'

'Yes. Although I wish that I didn't,' he said drily. Then, in a rather different tone of voice, he added, 'It will be for just a couple of days?'

Mae nodded. 'That's all—I promise.'

He gave a slightly frustrated grunt, but then told the driver the address of Mae's flat. When the taxi finally pulled up outside, he made no effort to get out and carry in her suitcase for her.

'If I once set foot inside that flat, I might not be able to make myself leave,' he said wryly. 'But I'll be back in two days' time,' he warned.

The taxi pulled away, leaving Mae to trudge inside. She dropped her case in the corner and made no attempt to unpack it. Then she stretched out on the bed, closed her eyes, and almost immediately went to sleep.

She slept on and off for nearly forty-eight hours, waking up only for an occasional drink, or to nibble at a light snack. It was almost as if she had been through a long illness, and needed time to recuperate before resuming her normal life. She knew she ought to be thinking about going back to work, finding a way of telling her mother what had happened, coming to terms with her new relationship with Lyndon. Instead, she just slept, deliberately not thinking about anything at all, so that her mind and body had time to rest.

When she woke up on the third morning, her head was clear and she could feel all her old energy returning. A very cool shower completed her revival, and then she wriggled into jeans and a T-shirt.

She raided her small freezer, and cooked herself a huge breakfast, to make up for all the meals she had missed over the last couple of days. She had just finished eating and was about to clear away the plates when the doorbell rang.

Mae felt her heart give a distinct thud, and it was still beating much harder than usual when she opened the door.

Lyndon was standing on the other side, looking outwardly relaxed, but with a rather bright light in his eyes.

'Your two days are up,' he told her softly. 'I've come to get you.'

She swallowed hard. 'Where—where are you going to take me?'

'Back to my flat. I want you there when I come home at night, there if I ring during the day. You can sleep in the spare bedroom, if you like. I'll get pretty frustrated, but I can live with that as long as I know you're under my roof. And you'll move out of the spare bedroom, of course, as soon as we make the whole thing legal.'

Mae gulped again. 'How—how legal?'

'*Very* legal,' he said firmly. 'And you'd better realise right now that this is going to last a lifetime. I don't like divorce, or families being split up. If you've any doubts about this, you'd better tell me right now. Once you come with me, it'll be too late.'

'I haven't any doubts,' Mae found herself saying in an astonishingly firm voice. Was that the truth? she wondered. She supposed it had to be! Just as she supposed that she was meekly about to let Lyndon drag her back to his flat.

'I think I ought to warn you that we'll be moving fairly soon,' he told her. 'The lease on the flat runs out next month, and I can't afford to renew it. And we'll be going somewhere rather more downmarket,' he went on drily. 'A journalist earns good money, but not enough to afford a flat in one of the most expensive areas of London. And the car will probably have to go, as well.'

'It doesn't matter,' she said cheerfully. 'It was far too flashy, anyway.'

Lyndon was already opening cupboards and drawers. 'What do you want to bring with you?' he asked.

She began to pull out clothes and personal belongings. 'Not very much. It should all go into a couple of suitcases.' Then she suddenly straightened up and looked at him. 'That's all you'll be getting,' she said in an even tone. 'Just me. Not Malcolm Morgan's daughter—not an heiress. Even if he were to have a miraculous change of heart and try to give me some of his money, I wouldn't take it.'

'I wouldn't *let* you take it,' Lyndon said, his light blue eyes boring straight into hers. 'I won't accept another man's money. But I will take his daughter,' he added in a softer tone. 'And I'll keep her, for the rest of my life.'

Neither of them said anything for several long moments. They just stood there looking at each other, blue gaze locked on to yellow.

'I'm fighting the temptation to kiss you,' Lyndon said at last, his mouth relaxing into a faint grin. 'But if I do, we might never get out of here.'

'I think I'd like you to kiss me, all the same,' Mae said in a small voice.

He gave a resigned shrug. 'How can I possibly turn down an invitation like that?'

His mouth was warm, hard and possessive. His kisses became increasingly demanding, until both of them were out of breath and a little shaken. He made no other attempt to touch her, though, as if he knew that just one small caress would be enough to push both of them beyond the point where any sort of control was possible.

At last, with a dark grimace, he pushed her gently away from him. 'Enough!' he muttered. 'Much more of this, and I'll feel frustrated for the rest of the week!'

Mae was too hot and flustered to say anything at all. To take her mind off the sweet ache that had spread right through her body, she began stuffing her belongings into a couple of suitcases. It was only when she had finished packing that she turned back to Lyndon.

'I'm ready to leave now.'

He looked at her hard for a moment. 'You're absolutely sure you want to do this? Once you walk out that door with me, it'll be too late to change your mind.'

'I'm sure,' she said without hesitation.

His mouth relaxed. 'Then let's get going.'

Once outside, he tossed her cases into the boot of his car. Then he opened the door, so she could get in. As she slid into the front seat, though, Mae suddenly looked up at him.

'I don't think I can go straight to your flat,' she told him.

His blue gaze darkened a fraction. 'Why not?'

'There's something else I've got to do first.'

'What?' he asked.

'I've got to go and see my mother.'

He kept looking at her steadily for a few moments. Then he nodded. 'I think that would be a good idea. I'll take you there. She lives in Kent, doesn't she?'

'Yes. She runs a small antique shop. If you head southwards out of London, I'll give you directions.'

He slid into the driving seat and the car purred off softly, the powerful engine easing it through the congested traffic. Mae was very quiet, and Lyndon finally glanced at her.

'You're not looking forward to this meeting, are you?' he guessed shrewdly.

'No, I'm not. I told you that she would never even talk about my father. And now I've got to go and tell her that I've actually met him.'

'Why don't you let me tell her?' he suggested.

Mae looked at him in astonishment. 'You?'

'Sometimes, it's easier to talk to a stranger. Let me go and break the news to her. Then, when she's calmed down, you can come in and fill in some of the details.'

'No, I can't let you do that,' she said regretfully. 'I don't know how she's going to react. It might all get very fraught and emotional.'

'I've never met your mother,' said Lyndon, 'but, from what you've told me about her, she doesn't sound like the hysterical type. And even if the situation does get rather difficult, I can handle it.'

'No, it wouldn't be fair,' Mae said, after a long pause. 'It's my problem. There's no reason for you to get involved in it.'

At that, he shot her an unexpectedly fierce glance. 'I *am* involved,' he reminded her. 'If it weren't for me, you'd never have met your father. I was the one who took you to Lindos, and forced you to go through with that meeting with him.'

'You didn't really force me into anything. Once I knew his name, knew that there was a chance of finding out something about him, I had to go ahead and see him. All right, so it turned out he was a pretty unpleasant man and I didn't actually like him, but even that was better than knowing nothing at all.'

Lyndon was silent for some time. Then he said, 'I'd still like to break the news to your mother. I've got to meet her at some time. It might as well be now.'

Mae shook her head indecisively. 'I don't know— I'll make up my mind when we get there.'

A little under an hour later, they had left the suburbs of London behind, and were driving through countryside that was lit by the golden sunshine of late summer. They passed through tiny villages, sleepy and quiet, and finally reached a small town.

'This is it,' said Mae with growing nervousness. 'My mother's shop is at the far end of the High Street.'

There was an empty parking space just outside. Lyndon pulled into it, and then cut the engine.

Mae looked at the familiar sign over the shop: 'Stanfield Antiques'. She couldn't see any customers inside. It was early afternoon by now, though, which was usually a fairly slack time.

She started to open the car door. Then she suddenly closed it again. She was positively shaking inside. There was no way she could go through with this.

'I can't go into that shop,' she said abruptly. 'I want to go back to London. Please take me back.'

'We've come this far,' Lyndon said calmly. 'There's no point in running away now. Let me go and speak to her.'

Mae twisted her fingers together indecisively. 'I don't think that's a very good idea——' she muttered.

'It's an excellent idea,' he said firmly. Then he looked directly at her. 'Trust me, Mae.'

She gazed back into his familiar light blue eyes. Then she nodded. 'All right. And I *do* trust you,' she added quietly.

He leant towards her and gave her a quick, light kiss. Then he got out of the car and walked into the shop.

Mae saw her mother coming over to meet him, thinking that he was just a customer. Lyndon spoke to her at some length. Then the two of them disappeared into the private room at the rear of the shop.

She sat in the car and nervously nibbled her nails, something she hadn't done for years. It began to seem as if Lyndon had been in that shop forever, although it was probably much less than half an hour.

At long last, he came out again. Mae's stomach lurched uncomfortably as he got back into the car.

'How did she take it?' she asked in a shaky voice.

'Not too well, at first,' Lyndon admitted. 'She's certainly built up a lot of hatred and resentment towards your father, over the years. That's hardly surprising, though, considering the way he treated her. She finally agreed that you had the right to know something about the man who had fathered you, though. And she doesn't blame you for going to see him and trying to find out the truth.'

Mae slumped back into her seat with relief. 'You must have been very persuasive! I suppose you kept radiating all that charm at her, and eventually she just melted away.'

'The same way that you melted?' he said, with a sudden grin.

'I suppose so,' she said with a wry answering smile. Then she looked at him. 'Should I go in and see her?'

'I think that you should.'

'Will you come with me?'

Lyndon shook his head. 'It would be best if you went on your own this time. But I'll be here, waiting for you.'

Mae slowly got out of the car and walked towards the shop. When she reached the door, she stopped for a moment. Then she took a deep breath and went inside.

Her mother was standing at the far end of the shop. She looked at Mae as she came in. Then she lifted one eyebrow in a wry expression.

'There's no need to look quite so scared,' she told her daughter. 'I'm not angry any more. I'm not going to bite your head off.'

Mae sagged with relief. 'I know that I should have told you all about it before I went whizzing off to the Greek islands,' she said apologetically. 'But everything happened so fast, there didn't seem time, and anyway——'

'You didn't have the nerve,' her mother finished for her.

'No, I didn't,' she admitted. Then she looked a little anxious again. 'You didn't mind that Lyndon was the one who told you what I've been doing these last few days?'

'When he first began to explain why he was here, I was very, very angry,' her mother said frankly. 'I demanded to know what right he had to interfere in such personal matters.'

'What did he say?' asked Mae rather apprehensively.

'That he didn't really have any right at all—except for the fact that I was about to become his mother-in-law.'

Mae gulped. 'Oh—yes—that's something else I should have told you about.'

'It seems that you've had a very interesting few days,' her mother said drily. 'Are there any more shocks that I should prepare myself for?'

'Well——' Mae licked her lips nervously, and tried again. 'I've been thinking about it, and I've got the feeling that Malcolm Morgan—my father—might try to get in touch with you.'

To her surprise, her mother didn't react as strongly as she had expected.

'Yes, I think that's a possibility,' she agreed after a long pause.

'What—what will you say to him?'

'I'll probably ask him what right he has to come barging back into my life, after the appalling way he behaved all those years ago.' Her mother's voice was more flat now. 'What did you think of your father?' she asked, after a few moments' silence.

'I didn't like him,' Mae admitted reluctantly. 'He doesn't seem to be interested in anything very much except money. He's definitely got a warped sense of values. I shouldn't think that he's at all an easy man to love.'

'He was easy to love once,' her mother said rather abruptly. 'I suppose he's changed over the years.'

Mae looked at her mother. Then she said hesitantly, 'You do know why he threw you out, don't you?'

'It was because he was tired of me, I suppose,' her mother said with fresh bitterness. 'Isn't that why men usually throw out their lovers?'

'No, it wasn't that.' She had suspected all along that her mother hadn't known the truth. How to tell her, though? Perhaps it would be best just to come out with it. Mae took a very deep breath. 'He didn't believe the baby you were expecting was his.'

'What?' A bright flush of colour swept over her mother's cheeks. Then she recovered a little. 'How do you know that? Did he tell you?' When Mae nodded, her mother's eyes flashed angrily. 'How could he possibly think it wasn't his?'

'Because he'd had a lot of tests and the doctors had told him he was infertile.' Mae waited for the shock to fade from her mother's face and then she went on, 'They said that there was less than a chance in a million he could ever father a child. When you told him you were pregnant, he was absolutely sure it couldn't be his. He was certain you'd been sleeping with someone else, and that you were trying to pass that other man's child off as his.'

'He *told* you this?' asked her mother incredulously.

'Yes.'

'But why didn't he tell *me*? Why did he just throw me out without any explanation at all?'

'I don't know,' Mae said softly. 'Unless, perhaps, he'd only just found out and couldn't talk about it, not to anybody. For most men, it must be a huge shock to be told they're infertile. They probably wouldn't want anyone to know about it.'

'But he told you,' her mother reminded her, her voice still bitter.

'He's a lot older now, a lot more mature. And he's had nearly twenty-five years to get used to the idea. I suppose he doesn't mind so much now if people know about it.'

Her mother was silent for a very long time. Then she said, 'Does he finally believe that you are his daughter?'

'Yes,' said Mae. Then she gave a very thin smile. 'I think it knocked him completely off balance when I turned up on Lindos. I'm that chance in a million—no one really expects those kind of odds to come up.'

Her mother sat down rather heavily. 'I need to think about this,' she said. 'I wasn't expecting anything like this ever to happen.'

'If he does come and see you—what will you do?' asked Mae.

'I don't know,' replied her mother. Then she looked at her daughter. 'He might want to see you, as well. What will *you* do?'

'When I left Lindos, I thought I never wanted to see him again,' Mae said slowly, after a long pause. 'But perhaps I only saw the worst side of him. Perhaps there is another side, a more likeable side. Maybe I ought to give him one more chance.'

They were both silent for some time. Then her mother said, 'I think I'd like to be on my own for a while. Perhaps you could ask that rather extraordinary man of yours to take you back to London. Come down and see me again in a couple of days, when we've all had time to think this over and come to terms with it.'

'All right,' said Mae, with a quick smile. They exchanged light kisses. Then they suddenly gave each other a much longer hug.

Mae finally left the shop feeling happy and relieved. She got into the car and gave Lyndon a big grin.

'Everything's all right?' he guessed.

'I think that everything is going to be very much all right. And my mother likes you. In fact, I get the impression that she's fallen for you in a big way. Although I don't suppose there are many women who *don't* like you,' she said drily.

'You didn't, when we first met,' he reminded her.

'I think that I did. It's just that I wouldn't admit it.'

'But you don't mind admitting it now?'

'No,' she said equably. 'But I'm not going to tell you too often, or you'll only get conceited.'

Lyndon switched on the engine, and then looked at her. 'Where do you want to go?' he asked. 'Back to my flat?'

'Why not?' she said. 'We might as well live in luxury while we can.'

He began to head the car back towards London. 'I could always write another book,' he said. 'With some luck, and the right publicity, it'll do as well as the first, and we can live in all the luxury we want.'

But Mae shook her head. 'You don't want to write another book. You want to be a journalist.'

'It would make a considerable difference to our lifestyle,' he pointed out.

'I don't want a "lifestyle". I just want to live with you and be happy.'

He raised one dark eyebrow. 'You're sure I can make you happy?'

'You've done pretty well, so far,' Mae said cheerfully. 'Oh, I'll admit there have been one or two low points, but on the whole you've been a great success.'

'If you carry on like this for much longer, you *will* make me conceited,' he said drily. They drove on for a while in comfortable silence, and then he turned and glanced at her. 'What do you want to do with the rest of your life, Mae?'

'Me?' she said, a little startled.

'I know you're working as a legal secretary, but do you want to carry on with your job? Do you enjoy it?'

'Yes, I do enjoy it,' she said. 'And it's quite demanding, but it doesn't stretch me quite as much as I'd like.'

'Have you ever thought of studying for a degree in law?' he suggested. 'If you're interested in the legal profession, then that would be a good first step.'

'Yes, I have thought about it a couple of times,' admitted Mae. 'But I wasn't sure I could do it.'

'Of course you could,' he said firmly. 'You're intelligent, and you stick at things.'

'You wouldn't mind? I mean, you're not against working wives?'

'I don't see why women should be expected to stay at home all day mending socks, polishing floors and slaving over hot stoves. You've got a good brain and you should use it.'

'What if we—well—have a family?' she said a little awkwardly. 'That's if you want to, of course.'

'I want to,' Lyndon said at once. 'I like kids. I hope we have at least a couple. But thousands of women raise a family with a lot of love and care, and manage a career at the same time. You're certainly clever enough to do it.'

Mae was quiet for a long time as she thought about it. She could still hardly believe that her life had changed so dramatically in such a short time. She had found her father, she was about to acquire a husband, and in the future there would be children—and a career, if she wanted it.

'I'm very glad I met you,' she said at last.

They were driving along a very quiet stretch of road, and Lyndon pulled the car into a deserted layby.

'How glad?' he said, with a wicked grin.

'*Very* glad,' she murmured, as she wriggled over so she could be closer to him.

A few minutes later, he grunted in frustration. 'I'm too old to be making love in a car!'

'How old are you?' she asked curiously.

'Thirty-one,' he said. 'Didn't you know that?'

'I never asked. In fact, there are a whole load of things I don't know about you.'

'Ask me at some other time,' he murmured. 'I've other things on my mind right now!'

His mouth returned to hers, and Mae sighed softly with pleasure. Her eyes were just fluttering shut when her gaze drifted over the driving-mirror. Then they shot open again and she hurriedly pushed away his hand, which was moving purposefully towards the softness of her breast.

'Stop it!' she hissed at him.

'I don't want to,' Lyndon said lazily. 'And I don't think you really want me to, either.'

'I don't,' she admitted. 'But a police car's just pulled into the layby behind us! I think they're going to come and ask us what we're doing.'

'I hope they don't blush, when I tell them,' said Lyndon, with a grin. 'And when they've finished checking my licence, perhaps we'll ask them for a police escort back to London. If I don't get you on your own fairly soon, I think it's seriously going to affect my health!'

Just at that moment, though, the police car pulled out again and disappeared off up the road.

'They obviously thought we looked innocent,' Lyndon remarked.

'I think that "innocent" is about the last word I'd ever use to describe you!' Mae said tartly. Then she let out a small squeak. 'Don't do that!'

'Why not?' he said, his blue eyes darkening. 'We're on our own now. Don't you like being alone with me?' he asked huskily.

Oh, yes, she liked it! She liked—loved—everything about this man. He moved towards her again, and Mae surrendered without a fight.

She was going to spend the rest of her life getting to know Lyndon Hyde, and she intended to enjoy every single minute of it—starting right now.

HARLEQUIN
Romance®

**HARLEQUIN ROMANCE
IS BETTING ON LOVE!**

And The Bridal Collection's
September title is a sure bet.

**JACK OF HEARTS (#3218)
by Heather Allison**

THE BRIDAL COLLECTION

THE BRIDE played her part.
THE GROOM played for keeps.
THEIR WEDDING was in the cards!

Available in August in
THE BRIDAL COLLECTION:

**THE BEST-MADE PLANS (#3214)
by Leigh Michaels**

Harlequin Romance

Wherever Harlequin
books are sold.

WED-5

WELCOME TO

The quintessential small town, where everyone knows everybody else!

Finally, books that capture the pleasure of tuning in to your favorite TV show!

GREAT READING... GREAT SAVINGS... AND A FABULOUS FREE GIFT!

Each book set in Tyler is a self-contained love story; together, the twelve novels stitch the fabric of the community. The covers honor the old American tradition of quilting; each cover depicts a patch of the large Tyler quilt.

With Tyler you can receive a fabulous gift, ABSOLUTELY FREE, by collecting proofs-of-purchase found in each Tyler book. And use our special Tyler coupons to save on your next TYLER book purchase.

Join your friends at Tyler for the seventh book, ARROWPOINT by Suzanne Ellison,
available in September.

Rumors fly about the death at the old lodge! What happens when Renata Meyer finds an ancient Indian sitting cross-legged on her lawn?
